COWBOY'S CHRISTMAS BRIDESMAID

TRINITY FALLS SWEET ROMANCE - ICICLE CHRISTMAS - BOOK 8

CLARA PINES

PINE NUT PRESS

Pine Nut Press

PO Box 506

Swarthmore, PA 19081

pinenutpress@gmail.com

Cover designed by The Book Brander

1

VALENTINA

Valentina slowed her pace when she reached Park Avenue, admiring the pretty storefronts all decorated for Christmas, and catching her breath a little at the end of her brisk morning walk.

Walking before work got her energy flowing and her mind ready to tackle whatever the day threw at her. Admittedly, she hadn't enjoyed dragging herself out of bed early at first, or bundling up to face the weather once it turned cold. But now that she was living in a little apartment in Trinity Falls village, Valentina had actually started looking forward to her morning burst of activity.

She didn't even mind the cold, since the scenery here at Christmastime was like something out of the movies she and her mom had watched together during every holiday season of her childhood. Sprawling Victorian houses were hung with twinkling lights, and some owners had even added lighting and decorations to the trees in their front yards.

But it wasn't just the way the town looked that made it

feel magical—it was the way neighbors greeted each other, asking about kids and parents, chatting about the weather and the upcoming Hometown Holiday celebration, or even just waving from across the street as they walked past with their dog or stroller. Even Valentina, who still knew practically no one, got a friendly wave or a *good morning* now and then.

Given her lofty career goals, she was pretty sure that she should feel stuck in this rural Pennsylvania town, but it seemed to be growing on her instead.

Until this year, Valentina had spent her life in a single-minded pursuit to become successful in the business world. Landing an internship with billionaire Sebastian Radcliffe had made her the envy of her business school class. She worked with him in Philadelphia for a few years, feeling incredibly lucky each time he took notice of her dedication and moved her up within the company.

Quickly, she became his right-hand-woman. And though he encouraged her to spin that role into something even bigger with another firm, she stuck around.

After all, she knew how rare it was to have a boss who didn't discount her ideas just because she was a woman, or because she had come from a modest background. Radcliffe was from a working-class family himself, and he always said it was a strength, not a weakness.

But when he essentially dropped everything to come to this little town and save it from developers by buying up land himself, he had offered her an out again, and it was possible she'd made a mistake by not taking it, at least in terms of advancing her career.

She was in her late twenties with a fancy degree and an impressive resume—poised to jump into the kind of project that was going to let her make her mark on the world. She was used to spending her days negotiating contracts and using her hard-earned, high-powered connections to make Radcliffe's enterprises run smoothly.

But today the highlight of her schedule would be a conversation with Randy, the elderly town building inspector, who would probably spend most of their allotted time showing her grainy photos of his great-grandson on his flip phone.

And yet somehow she felt happy. Snow flurries began to fall as she crossed the street to the café on the corner, and she smiled to herself at how much she felt like she was living in a tiny, perfect snow globe. She wanted to stick out her tongue and try to catch the tiny flakes, but obviously a grown woman couldn't do things like that in public.

The bells over the door of *Jolly Beans* jingled merrily as she pushed it open, releasing the rich scent of coffee and the owner's famous cranberry loaf.

"Hey, Valentina," Holly called out to her with a smile. "I'll be right over."

The friendly blonde waitress handed out the drinks and food from her tray to a table where two young moms sat with their toddlers, and then headed to the counter where Valentina waited with her insulated travel cup.

"The usual?" Holly asked.

Holly was one person in town who definitely knew

Valentina's name, since she grabbed her first cup of coffee each day here after her walk.

"Yes, please," she said. "And I'd love your help with something else today, too. Do you know what Randy Ullman likes as a snack? I'm meeting him later on."

"Isn't that sweet of you?" Holly said with a smile.

"Well, my dad always says *the way to a man's heart is through his stomach*," Valentina replied. "And Mr. Radcliffe is waiting for some permits to go through. I thought maybe Randy would take an extra moment just to go over everything with me if I have his favorite treat for him to enjoy while he does."

"Well, now that's practical *and* sweet," Holly told her. "Randy says the rich stuff doesn't agree with him, but I do notice he's partial to our raisin scones lately."

"Perfect," Valentina said. "I'll take two of those as well."

"You got it," Holly said, grabbing the tongs and bending to slide two of the fresh-baked treats into a paper bag.

Valentina looked around a little as Holly poured coffee into her reusable cup. The small café was bustling already, even though it was still early. Its location right next to the train station meant there were always commuters coming and going, and of course Trinity Falls had plenty of people up early to exercise, or with small kids. There were even a handful of local farmers here, probably grabbing a coffee before heading over to the hardware store.

And just like the neighbors out on their lawns, everyone here seemed to know each other. They called across the tables to say hello or stopped on their way past to exchange pleasantries.

"Valentina," a familiar voice said.

She felt a little spark of pleasure as she turned to see Caroline from the library. Even if it was only because of a community activity like a book club, it was really nice to have someone greet her, too.

"Hi, Caroline," she said. "How are you?"

"Great," Caroline said. "Looking forward to telling Pennsylvania ghost stories with the campers this weekend. The research was fun."

Caroline and her husband Logan had taken on a huge project this year, building cabins on the Williams family homestead to host kids from the city who wanted to come out and learn about farming, nature, and, if Caroline had anything to do with it, storytelling.

"I'm sure it will be magical," Valentina told her sincerely. "You do everything with your whole heart."

"Thanks," Caroline told her, looking gratified. "I'm lucky to get to do what I love."

Valentina smiled at that and felt a pang of... something, like thinking she should be missing that feeling herself since things had slowed so much for her lately. But even though it didn't make sense to her, she still felt happy.

"Here you go," Holly said from behind the counter.

Valentina thanked her and paid, saying her goodbyes to Caroline and still wondering what had gotten into her today. Sure, she liked Trinity Falls, but she really should want to be doing more with herself than trying to get her boss out of the pickle he was in with all the properties he had purchased.

She stood outside her car for a moment and took a sip of her coffee, savoring the delicious brew and the fresh, cold air.

I just need to shake off the morning cobwebs, she told herself as she got in the car, placing the bag with the scones on the passenger seat.

The drive from the village out to the farmhouse where Radcliffe based his operations was beautiful—just what she needed to clear her head. The tiny town melted quickly into pretty houses, and from there she passed the campus of the community college.

After that, she was driving past fields and farmhouses under a soft, cloudy gray sky. The road curved over and around small hillsides and past actual red barns, so that she felt like she was in a car commercial or something.

At last, she spotted the familiar sign for Whispering Ridge, and pulled up to park in the gravel driveway.

Radcliffe might have tied up a lot of his fortune in land, but he was still a billionaire. Valentina assumed that meant he could afford to pave the driveway, or remove the flowery wallpaper from the first floor of the house, which included his office and hers.

But the man had honestly been born for the country life. He chopped his own wood for the fireplace, and sometimes dressed like that was his whole job. The old-fashioned decor of the house didn't seem to bother him at all.

Luckily, his fiancée Emma, who Valentina liked very much, was a local, and she was about as formal as he was, so she didn't mind him looking like a lumberjack sometimes. They were a great couple, and Valentina was looking forward to being a bridesmaid at their upcoming wedding.

She hadn't really hit it off with Emma from day one, mostly due to Valentina's possibly overdeveloped sense of loyalty to her boss. But once she came to terms with the fact that Emma wasn't just one more woman chasing Radcliffe for his money, and the people in the little town really were as nice as they seemed, things got easier. And even though her stand-offishness had probably set her social standing back quite a bit with the rest of the town, she was able to forge a real friendship with Emma.

Valentina grabbed the sealed container she'd stowed in the trunk before her morning walk, as well as her coffee cup and the scones, and headed inside. She made her way quickly through the center hall, back to the sunny addition the former owners had called a *Florida room* and ducked into her office, where she slipped off her sneakers and put on a nice pair of heels.

While her boss could afford to come to work in denim and flannel, Valentina still followed her father's advice: *Dress for the job you want.* That meant business clothing, high heels, and her own fashion favorite—pretty, dangly earrings—every day.

She ran her finger once down the back of the small bronze statue of a horse that she kept on her desk. Her grandfather had bought it at a pawn shop more than fifty years ago. The day her dad passed it on to her, she vowed to keep it near her always.

Santiago Jimenez had always wanted to own a horse,

but he spent his lifetime working hard in the city to ensure that his son could get a great education. He had passed before Valentina was born, but she still felt like she knew him. Many of her dad's sayings came from him.

I see horses every day here, Abuelo, she told him in her mind. *You would love it.*

She tucked the bag of scones safely into a desk drawer. The crews she worked with were outside most of the day in cold weather, and it meant they were always ravenous, so no food was safe if it was visible.

Fortunately, that lined up perfectly with the fact that Valentina loved to bake. She grabbed the bigger container she brought in and her now-empty coffee cup and headed out the back door and down to the big barn, where most of the guys had coffee every morning before heading out on assignments.

Valentina held formal meetings with the crew bosses regularly to discuss their progress with the properties that were being renovated and resold. But she had found that she could learn more about day-to-day operations by standing around the coffee urn with the workmen than she ever could in an official meeting. And dropping off treats while she grabbed her second cup of coffee was a great way to get the team going.

Teetering down the slight hill in her heels was a small price to pay for good information. Thankfully, someone had laid some boards over the uneven gravel path at some point during her first year working here, so it was a lot easier to traverse now than it had been picking her way through mud and rocks in the beginning.

"Valentina," Daniel Sullivan said happily as she

"I have a meeting with Randy Ullman," she said. "Which I should probably get to now."

The guys sent her off with thanks for the treats and wishes of good luck for the meeting. They knew as well as she did that getting permits taken care of was a lot of work, and not always in her control.

She hoped that today she could at least get a road map of what needed to happen to close out four or five houses that she really thought should be just about ready.

As she was heading to the parking area to drive back into town, her cell phone rang. *Natalie Cassidy* appeared on the screen.

While Valentina and Emma had ultimately bonded, she wasn't close with Emma's other friends. She hoped she could make a good impression on them and maybe end the wedding with a handful of new friends after sharing bridesmaid duties together.

The phone call from Natalie was unusual, though—typically any bridesmaid news was shared in the group chat.

"Hi, Natalie," she said. "I'm getting in the car, so hang on for just a second."

"Sure," Natalie said happily.

"Okay, sorry about that," Valentina said, once she had the car started and the call switched over to the speaker. "How's it going?"

"I know you're working," Natalie said. "But I just wanted to call you really quickly about a little thing for the wedding."

"Okay," Valentina said. "What can I do?"

"It's a fun surprise for Emma," Natalie said, a smile in her voice. "You know how she loves the movie *The Princess and the Stable Boy*?"

"Of course," Valentina said, smiling at the memory of Emma's horror when Valentina admitted she hadn't seen it yet. Naturally, the two of them had watched the classic romcom the next time they both had a free evening.

"Well, you know how at the end, the princess's sisters all come riding up on horseback before her wedding?" Natalie asked.

"Sure," Valentina said, thinking back to the bevy of women with flowing hair riding horses up the mountainside with the romantic theme song playing.

"We're going to do that," Natalie said, giggling with excitement.

"Do what?" Valentina asked.

"We're going to ride up to join her on horseback," Natalie said. "She'll think we just disappeared, and then we'll ride up the hillside. It will be perfect."

"Wow," Valentina said, feeling a little nervous at the idea. As a city girl, she hadn't really spent a lot of time around horses.

"I already talked to Shane," Natalie said. "We can bring horses over from our place. You know how to ride, right?"

"Sure," Valentina said automatically, not wanting to put a damper on any of the plans Natalie seemed so excited about.

Valentina didn't actually know how to ride, but how hard could it be? You just had to get on and steer. And besides, she had always wanted to learn to ride, even though she was just a little more intimidated by real horses than the ones in the movies, now that she had seen some up close. At least she would be one step closer to fulfilling her grandfather's dream.

And it really didn't matter either way. There was no way she would be the one bridesmaid who ruined everything by not being able to do something that would make Emma really happy.

"That's great," Natalie said, and launched into a rundown of other things they were all planning.

Valentina tried to focus on everything else Natalie was saying as she headed back for the village. But she couldn't help thinking to herself that if she had some friends, real friends, her life might feel more balanced.

2

VALENTINA

Valentina smiled as Randy Ullman came ambling into the lobby of the borough office only a few minutes after their scheduled meeting time.

People in Trinity Falls didn't seem to get as hung up about punctuality as they did in the rest of the world. And it seemed to Valentina that Randy probably moved more slowly now than he had when he was a younger man, and maybe he hadn't gotten around to adjusting his schedule to accommodate it yet. The last time they met, he'd been almost half an hour late. Today's meeting was in the morning though, so maybe he hadn't had a chance to get as far behind yet.

She made a mental note to always try and schedule meetings with him for the morning.

"Hey there, sweetheart," Randy said with a kind smile.

She wasn't sure if he always used endearments like

that at work, or if he was maybe having trouble remembering her name, but she took no offense either way.

"Hi, Randy," she replied. "Thank you so much for making some time for me."

"Anytime," he said. "Let's go to the conference room so we can get off our feet."

She followed him back to the small room overlooking the parking lot. The sky was steel-gray now and some larger snowflakes were beginning to fall.

"Cold out there, eh?" Randy said, lowering himself carefully to his chair.

"Looks like real snow," she said, unable to help herself.

"Nah," Randy said, glancing over his shoulder. "Those are just little flurries. But just you wait. We'll get serious snow in January, and you won't be so excited about it."

He winked at her so she could tell he was just teasing. She didn't have the heart to remind him that she'd been here last winter, and aside from the big blizzard that shut down the whole town for a day or two, she hadn't really been too bothered by the snow.

"I hope you don't mind," she said. "But I brought us both a little breakfast. I never have a chance to eat in the mornings."

"Radcliffe keeps you busy, eh?" Randy said, chuckling.

"Coke Zero, right?" she asked, pulling the two cans she'd gotten from the machine out of her bag.

"Yes," he said happily, taking his. "Thanks a lot."

"And I got us each a raisin scone at *Jolly Beans* this morning," she told him as she set out the paper bag.

"Those are my favorite," he said, sounding surprised.

"Holly mentioned that you liked them when I told her I was planning to see you today," she admitted. "So I grabbed us a couple."

"What are you buttering me up for?" Randy asked her with a mischievous grin as he reached for his scone.

"I'm new to all this," Valentina said honestly. "But I really want to get everything done right. I was hoping we could just go over a handful of houses with open permits and you could let me know exactly what we should do to get ourselves in shape."

"You want to know what's taking so long," Randy said, understanding immediately what she was trying to say in her own polite way.

"Yes," she said, feeling relieved.

"Those houses in the valley aren't cleared yet because of the electrical," he told her simply. "You have a few smaller things, like missing smoke detectors here and there, but all of that could be done in a day or so. The only big thing on your plate right now is electrical."

"I see," she said, nodding.

"It's understandable," Randy said. "You just fired your electrician."

She was still amazed at just how fast word got around in the small town.

"He was cutting corners," Valentina said simply. "We don't cut corners."

Randy nodded, his eyes appreciative, but his mouth was full, so he didn't answer.

"Our new guy has been on the job for a week though," Valentina went on. "And he came highly recommended. If you don't mind taking a peek when you're down there looking at the roofing on 308, it should be done."

"I was at 308 for the heater yesterday," Randy said. "Electrical hasn't been touched."

It took all her years of business school training and work experience for Valentina to keep her face neutral.

What in heaven's name had Tanner Williams been doing all week?

She had tried not to wince when Radcliffe said Emma was recommending her cousin to step in and handle the electrical work. The man did have a great reputation in town. Valentina had checked on that herself before following Radcliffe's instruction to hire him.

But this kind of thing was what too often happened when you hired friends and family. They thought they were doing you a favor by taking on extra work or giving you a good price, but then they decided that meant the rules were different for them, and your job often got pushed off.

"Thank you for letting me know," she told him.

"He'll work at his own pace," Randy advised.

That wasn't something she'd heard about Tanner before now, but she took note. Randy had been handling inspections for decades. He knew his business, and in her experience he was pretty prone to doing things at his own pace himself. So if he had noticed Tanner was going slowly, it really meant something.

"I'll talk to him," she said, mentally already halfway to the valley to do so.

But then Randy cracked his soda can open and she

remembered that she had to actually sit and eat with him.

"You don't have to wait around," he said, smiling at her fondly. "I know you like to stay moving."

"I've been looking forward to having breakfast with you all day," she told him, cracking her own can open, her mouth watering at the hiss. "No way am I leaving without trying your favorite scones."

"We'll make a hometown girl of you yet, Valentina," he declared, surprising her by remembering her name and by lifting his can to clink hers.

"How are the grandkids?" she asked, as she took a bite of her scone. She had expected it to be flavorless and dry, but it melted in her mouth and the tiny raisins were sweet and delicious.

"I was going to try not to show you photos this time," Randy said a little sadly. "I really was. But Megan played a rutabaga in the school play last week and it really feels like you'd be missing out on something you don't get to see every day."

"I *definitely* want to see that," Valentina laughed, delighted to find that she meant it.

HALF AN HOUR LATER, she found that she was in great spirits heading into the countryside for the second time in one morning.

Randy wasn't wrong, she did like to stay moving. But taking a moment to connect once in a while really was nice. Just laughing with him over Megan's adorable photos in the rutabaga costume had been worth sacrificing a little bit of her morning.

And before she left, he'd casually offered her a huge favor.

"You're a good kid," he'd declared, leaning back and patting his belly. "If you want to start taking photos of the work, you can text them to me and I'll take a look and let you know in advance if I see problems."

He'd scrawled his cell number on a scrap of paper for her while she watched in total awe.

"Of course, I still have to see everything in person before I sign off," he told her sternly as he handed over the precious scrap of paper.

She had thanked him profusely, unable to believe her good fortune. Since Randy was part-time these days, she often had to wait days or weeks for an inspection depending on his schedule, only for him to require a small change that led to more waiting for a re-inspection. Sending photos in advance might make any project happen weeks faster if it let them get to work on his changes sooner.

She was sure he never would have offered if they hadn't shared breakfast today. But she decided the time spent would have been worth it either way.

Valentina was feeling good as she pulled up at the house where Tanner Williams had told her he'd be working today.

Their text exchange before she headed out had been straightforward and simple—she asked where he was, and within five minutes he responded. A lot of the crew didn't carry their phones while they were working, or didn't often stop in the middle of something to respond to them, so she was encouraged that he clearly made an effort to be reachable.

She hadn't been too pleased to hear that he was still at the big farmhouse on Juniper Lane though. The last guy had finished this place in a few days. Surely Tanner could have cleaned it up in a day or two.

She pulled up out front, admiring the great big house with the wide front porch, surrounded by what seemed to her like endless rolling acres.

If I ever settled down in the country, I'd want a house just like this one, she thought to herself.

Shaking her head at her own nonsense, Valentina headed carefully for the front porch. She didn't want to settle down in the country. She had no idea where such a funny thought would come from.

Wiping her feet on the towel someone had thoughtfully put down, she knocked on the door and then opened it.

"Hello," she called out as she stepped into the center hall.

Valentina had learned that you didn't wait for anyone to come to the door in a work zone. Half the time, the guys were up to their ears in a project in a remote part of the house, or using machinery that meant they couldn't hear the door anyway. Electricians did a lot of their work in basements and attics, so she expected she'd have to go looking for Tanner.

"Hey," a deep voice said from the doorway to the living room before she could take another step.

She almost jumped out of her shoes, but managed to steady herself.

"Sorry," he said with a half-smile. "I came up when you texted that you were on your way."

He was tall, with wide shoulders and dark hair. As he gazed down at her with crystal blue eyes, she had to admit to herself that he was annoyingly handsome. Faded jeans and a formfitting black sweater only added to his appeal.

"Valentina Jimenez," she said, sticking her hand out as she put herself into professional mode.

"Very nice to meet you, Miss Jimenez," he said, correctly pronouncing it *heem-AYN-ehz* like she did, instead of copping out and calling her Miss Valentina, like so many people did. "Tanner Williams."

He listens, a little voice in the back of her head noted with satisfaction as he took her hand. *And he looks like Prince Charming from one of those princess movies.*

An annoying shiver of awareness went through Valentina as their hands touched and she ended the handshake more quickly than she normally would have.

"Valentina's fine," she said, trying to stay professional. "I'm here to discuss the progress you're making on this project."

"None," he said simply.

"What do you mean?" she asked.

"I mean that the guy you had in here before was a slob," Tanner replied with quiet confidence. "I'm not making any progress of my own because I have to redo what he already did before I can start anything new."

"Howie Linck completed this house in four days," she

said. "Are you really telling me it's taking you over a week just to clean it up?"

"Yes," he said simply. "Probably two weeks."

Horror swept through her as she thought about what that was going to mean for the project timeline if it were true.

"You don't have two weeks," she told him firmly, determined to stay calm and professional. "We've got half a dozen properties waiting for electrical work to close out the permits. We hired you because you were supposed to be good. You were supposed to catch us up."

"I am good," he told her matter-of-factly. "But I'm not a magician."

Something about the cocky way he threw out the sarcastic remark broke down the last of her patience.

"I know you're Emma's cousin," she heard herself say, her voice anything but level as she marched toward him. "But that doesn't mean you can take advantage of Mr. Radcliffe and put his project on the back burner—"

"Miss Jimenez," he interrupted.

"Our boss did something very special for this town," she went on, ignoring his rude attempt to cut her off and grabbing the threshold of the living room doorway with one hand and placing her other hand on her hip as she settled in to give him a much-needed piece of her mind. "As far as I'm concerned everyone in this place should be grateful to him for what he did here."

"We definitely are, but—" he tried again.

"Instead," she went on, "I seem to have a string of electricians who only want to take his money and waste his time. Are you one of them, Tanner Williams? Is that what you're so anxious to tell me?"

"No, ma'am," he said right away when she was finished. "I was just trying to tell you that you're leaning in wet paint."

She blinked at him, and he pointed at her left arm, which rested against the molding. Pulling it away, she found that it was completely covered in white paint.

"There's a slop sink in the laundry room," Tanner offered. "But that's trim paint. I don't think it's coming out."

Closing her eyes, she counted to three as she took a deep breath and let it out. It was only a jacket. She loved this lavender skirt suit, but she had plenty of other outfits.

"I'm sorry," he said gently.

"It's fine," she said, opening her eyes and trying not to touch the rest of herself with the painty arm.

"I'm as grateful to Baz as anyone here," Tanner said. "He's done great things for the town, and he and his boy make my baby cousin really happy. That's exactly *why* I won't rush this project. His name is on these deeds, just like my name is on the work. You can have this kind of work done fast, or you can have it done right."

"I'm not asking you to cut corners," she said quickly.

"This house was powered with knob and tube wiring *throughout*," Tanner said. "That old wiring is a dangerous fire hazard. So nearly every wall in the house needs to have holes put in it and new wiring needs to be fed through. It's probably a two-week job, it definitely can't be done in four days. Linck did about a quarter of it, just the stuff that's easy to reach and see, conveniently."

Valentina nodded, that tracked from what she knew of the other electrician.

"So, in addition to cleaning up what he did in the panel and the walls, I'm running three-way switches and working in the crawlspaces," Tanner went on, running a hand through his hair and unconsciously showing off the muscles in his upper arm. "I'm doing all the spots that are harder to reach, where you sometimes have to get creative. And that takes time."

Valentina swallowed, shaking her head. This wasn't the news she wanted, but it really seemed like she was dealing with someone else who cared about their work.

She looked up at him, allowing herself to make more eye contact than she normally did with the guys, just to be sure he was telling her the truth.

His blue eyes flashed with ice and her breath caught in her throat. Why did he have to be so handsome? It certainly wasn't making this any easier. And why was she reacting to him like this? It wasn't like there weren't plenty of cute guys in Trinity Falls. But she'd never met one that was quite so distracting before. If she wasn't careful, he might get the wrong idea...

"Do you want to spend the night in this house tonight?" he asked, his deep voice sending a shiver through her.

What did he just ask me? the last sensible bone in her body demanded indignantly as she stood there frozen. *How dare he——*

"Because I won't leave this property until *I* would spend the night in it," he finished.

"Understood," she said, nodding and tearing her eyes from his. "Thank you for giving me the background. I'll let you get back to work, but please keep me apprised house by house as you finish each one up."

He stood there for a moment and she wondered if she had finally surprised him instead of the other way around.

"And I'd like you to take a look at the other properties," she added. "We should have a sit-down in the next few days to make a realistic schedule. I want things done right, without any corners cut. But I also expect you to keep an aggressive pace."

She turned to go, crushed that her whole schedule had just gone out the window, but glad that Radcliffe wasn't going to unknowingly sell houses with bad electrical work done to them. The first thing she was doing when she got back to the office was to check to be sure none of the homes Linck worked on had been sold yet. Fortunately, he'd only been with them for a month or so before she had realized his work wasn't up to par.

"Hang on, Miss Jimenez," Tanner called out to her suddenly when she had nearly reached the front door.

"Yes?" she said, turning back to him.

"You're going to get paint all over your car," he said, shaking his head.

"I can't meet with Mr. Radcliffe wearing a camisole," she said with a frown.

Tanner looked confused.

"It's like a tank top," she told him, suddenly wanting to giggle. "Women wear them under a blazer."

Before she knew what was happening, he was peeling off his sweater, revealing a slim-fitting Henley underneath. He was so strong, and she could tell those muscles were from real work, not from the gym.

"Here," he said, tossing her the sweater. "It's not fancy, but it's better than a paint-covered jacket, right?"

She definitely didn't have time to get all the way back to the village to change clothes before her meeting with Radcliffe.

"Thanks," she said.

He nodded to her, but didn't leave.

Is he waiting for me to take off my blazer?

The idea gave her an odd tingle that made her angry with herself. What on earth was happening to her? She'd never been boy-crazy. In fact, she had never really even dated. There just hadn't been time.

"Sorry," he said, seeming to realize she was waiting for him to leave. "I'll be in touch when I'm ready for that meeting."

"Fine," she said.

She waited until he had disappeared further into the house before unbuttoning her jacket and slipping it off.

His sweater was still toasty warm from his body heat, and it smelled delicious—like a wood fire, and spicy too, like maybe he wore old-fashioned aftershave. It felt like she was being held by the kind of man who knew how to fish and hunt and set up a campsite—all things she had absolutely zero interest in.

Get it together, she told herself fiercely.

She marched herself out of the house and back out to her car. But before she got in, she stopped and looked up at the two-story home one more time, and a strange sensation went through her as his words echoed in her head.

I won't leave this property until I would spend the night in it.

Mr. Radcliffe was in good hands with an electrician who had a sense of pride in his work—that must be why she felt a flutter of pleasure in her chest as she looked back at the house.

It was just professional satisfaction. That was all.

3

TANNER

Tanner Williams stood in the living room of the house on Juniper Lane, feeling completely out of sorts and wondering what on earth had just happened.

One minute he'd been elbows deep in the electrical panel, and the next... well, the woman who was essentially his boss had come clicking in on those heels like a hurricane, yelling about timelines and almost immediately covering herself in wet paint.

She had given the impression over text and email that she was one of those unflappable people—calm, level-headed, asking only the proper questions about licenses and references. But meeting her in person had certainly shown that she was more complicated.

Tanner smiled as he thought about the brief meeting. The look on her face when she realized he'd only been trying to save her outfit was priceless. Yet he hadn't been glad she messed up her nice clothes. He liked her right away, even when she was yelling at him.

It wasn't difficult. There was a lot to like about her. She was so earnest, and she seemed to actually care about her work. She was also so much younger than he'd thought she would be, and...

Don't you dare notice that she's beautiful, he told himself inwardly.

But he couldn't deny that when she looked up at him, he'd been thrown by the sweetness in her eyes.

And when she yelled at him, she was only doing it for Radcliffe's sake. Tanner liked that she was furious at the injustice of anyone not doing their best work for someone who had shown himself to be a selfless man.

Loyalty, he thought to himself.

The world could do with a whole lot more of that, as far as Tanner was concerned.

He shook his head and headed back down to work, not wanting to let his thoughts spin out to his ex-wife and her lack of loyalty. There was no point in that, especially when he was feeling good.

He grabbed the handrail of the basement stairs and gave it a nice shake, but it held firm. The fifteen minutes he'd put into it yesterday had paid off.

These were the tasks you didn't anticipate in a big project, but that were necessary. With everything he'd be carrying up and down, he couldn't risk a flimsy handrail. And besides, the borough inspector would check the handrails before Radcliffe could close on the property anyway.

But of course no one listened when you mentioned peripherals coming up on an estimate or a timeline.

Valentina listened, a little voice in the back of his head whispered.

It was true. He'd been amazed when she stopped and heard him out, thanked him for the background, and actually asked for another meeting to get his insights.

Lately it seemed like no one was listening—even his son's second grade teacher, who seemed to be set on the idea that Zeke and the other kids needed to do huge amounts of homework every night.

Tanner had taken the time to sit down and write her a polite email after the second week of school, letting her know that the homework was too much for little kids, especially all the math, and that his son really needed time outdoors after sitting in school all day.

The teacher shot back an email so quickly that he was pretty sure she just copied and pasted it without even really reading his message. She said she understood that the kids didn't like having homework, but that at this stage, they needed to *drill.*

Tanner could only roll his eyes. After a day of hard work and school, he and Zeke needed to go hiking or bike riding after school to unwind sometimes, not do a hundred math problems.

Besides, in Tanner's opinion, all those hours of *drilling* were a surefire way to guarantee that Zeke would hate math.

Tanner used math all day every day himself, doing load calculations, taking measurements, and writing up client estimates. Back in school he had been considered very good at math, and he had enjoyed solving more complex problems too.

But math had been math back then, not this endless catalogue of weird word problems and *drilling*.

It was stuff like this that made him miss having someone to vent to. This problem might not have a solution, but at least when Karen was around they could commiserate.

I'm better off without her, he reminded himself. And he knew it was true. He'd seen the spark go out with her years ago. They had married young, and Zeke had been a surprise blessing. Tanner adjusted quickly, and was awed and grateful to be a father. But it was pretty clear now that Karen hadn't been ready. At the end of the day, it was better to just have her gone than sticking around and phoning it in, even if it left him feeling like he was on his own.

The only other person he'd ever really liked talking to about problems was his brother, Axel. And he found himself longing for those times more and more lately. But Axel had taken off after high school graduation and barely came home anymore these days.

Tanner made it all the way to the panel before remembering that he couldn't continue what he'd been doing anyway. He needed to run to the supply shop for GFCI breakers.

Valentina Jimenez, you really threw me for a loop.

He even liked her name. Something about it was like music. For the first time in what felt like forever, he itched to get out his dad's old guitar and noodle around on it.

By the time he was in his truck and heading down the farmhouse's long driveway, he was feeling more like himself than he had in a long time. He'd rolled one window partly down, letting in an icy blast of fresh air and snow flurries as Bing Crosby sang "Winter Wonderland" on the radio.

Tanner had always loved the farmland that stretched between his aunt and uncle's place and Route One. The little hills and crests looked like something out of a movie, especially when they were covered in snow, as they soon would be.

Everyone knew it didn't really snow much here until January, but Tanner had a hunch this year. He could taste it on the air. And there were so many flurries lately. That had to mean something. He had always loved the snow, even if it was a pain to shovel out sometimes. And Zeke was already asking about sledding.

Twenty minutes later, Tanner was singing along to "The Twelve Days of Christmas" as he pulled into the parking lot of Singh Lighting & Electrical Supplies.

The main showroom was full of chandeliers. Tanner normally hated having to duck to get past all of it, praying not to knock down any of the pricey crystal concoctions as he made his way back to the supply counter. He couldn't help noticing the prices from the dangling tags, and he definitely couldn't afford to smash anything.

But today, there seemed to be some new magic in the shimmering chandeliers and he paused in the center of them all, feeling like he was floating in the sky in the middle of a cloud of fireflies, or maybe an ice storm.

It's beautiful, he realized. *And it reminds me of something...*

But he wasn't really sure what, at first. He'd only

installed a handful of these things in his career. Folks in Trinity Falls normally asked for simpler fixtures.

Valentina's earrings.

He thought of the long, shimmering earrings flashing when she shook her head and couldn't keep himself from grinning. His boss wore earrings so crazy that a giant showroom full of chandeliers made him think of her.

Yet in spite of the sparkling earrings and the clicking heels, there was an innocence about her. The shy way she had looked at him when he tossed her his sweater—like she was grateful and nervous at the same time—came back to him suddenly and he remembered the spark he'd felt when they shook hands, almost like he'd grabbed onto a live wire.

Had she felt it too?

"Tanner," Mr. Singh said fondly, approaching him from the main counter where he had been talking with a customer when Tanner walked in. "Were you here to talk about fixtures today?"

"No, no," Tanner said. "Just supplies."

"Oh," Mr. Singh said, sounding surprised. And Tanner could hardly blame him, since he'd been standing in the middle of the chandeliers looking around like he expected them to start talking or something.

Tanner headed back to the supply counter, where Mr. Singh's son, Dev, sat, typing away on a laptop.

"Hey, Dev," Tanner said.

"Hi, Tanner," Dev returned. "How's it going?"

Tanner explained what he needed, and Dev headed back, grabbing things from what always seemed to Tanner like thousands of shelves, without even looking at the tags. Of course, Dev had grown up in the shop, but it was still impressive. In just a minute or two, he came back to Tanner with a big grin on his face.

"I know you're not an impulse buyer," he said to Tanner, placing his items on the counter. "But today I have some stuff that's actually sort of practical."

Tanner waited while the teenager pulled a box out from under the counter. Dev used part of the wages his parents paid him to buy returned packages from a warehouse store. Then he resold the items from the shop or on an online auction site.

Tanner figured it was an enterprising activity for the kid, even if most of what he bought he probably ended up donating or throwing away.

"Work coveralls," Dev said proudly, placing the box on the counter.

Tanner hated to break it to the kid, but he worked in jeans and flannels or sweaters for the most part, and he didn't mind them getting dirty.

But a bit of pale purple fabric peeked out from among the others.

"You have a purple one?" he heard himself ask.

"Lilac," Dev said, sounding a little surprised as he pulled it out and handed it to Tanner.

It was the same shade as the suit Valentina had been wearing. She probably could use something like this if she wanted to visit work sites all the time.

"How much?" he asked.

Dev answered with a reasonable number, and Tanner nodded.

"You have to pay for this separately," Dev said.

"Of course," Tanner told him, handing over cash for the coverall and then putting the supplies on his business account.

As he headed back out to his truck with his purchases, he felt a funny jolt of happiness at the idea of giving Valentina his little gift, even if it was only a work thing, and practical.

You're just happy to work for someone who listens, he told himself firmly. *It's natural to be excited about that.*

It was only feeling good about a lucky break at work. That was all.

4

VALENTINA

Valentina tugged at the borrowed sweater and pushed the sleeves up around her elbows again so that she would look less like a child dressing up in her father's clothing.

Her meeting today with Radcliffe was an important one. She couldn't have him distracted by what she was wearing. And she didn't want herself to be distracted by thinking about how effortlessly Tanner's muscular frame had filled out the garment when he'd been wearing it.

"I like your sweater," Radcliffe's voice boomed from the back door to the offices.

She should have known he would notice immediately.

"Uh, thanks," she said, wondering if he was being sincere.

But he wore a genuine smile, and she was reminded, yet again, that her boss sometimes teased in a friendly way, but he was never sarcastic or hurtful.

"Now if we can just get you into some comfortable

shoes, I might feel like this adventure in the country has done you some good," Radcliffe added, winking.

"These are comfortable," she said lightly.

She honestly wasn't sure anymore if her heels were comfortable or not. It was just that she was used to them and they made her feel professional, which was its own kind of comfort. Besides, she was on the short side to begin with, and all the men here seemed to be as big as lumberjacks. Her heels helped her feel like she was at least a little closer to their level.

"Come on in," Radcliffe said. "Mrs. Luckett brought over some blueberry muffins this morning."

"I had breakfast with the borough inspector already," she said. "But thank you."

"A productive morning," Radcliffe said, his eyebrows lifting like he was impressed. "Don't you ever do anything just for fun, Valentina? I hope I don't make you feel like you can't."

"It *was* fun," she said. "I saw photos of his grand-daughter dressed up like a rutabaga."

"That's adorable," Radcliffe said. "I remember when Wes played a carrot in his school play."

"Me too," Valentina said, smiling.

Radcliffe's son was such a nice boy. She was glad for his sake that they had left the city. Wes really seemed to be thriving out here. And Radcliffe was marrying into a family with a lot of cousins for him to socialize with.

"So, it seems like we're chugging along," Radcliffe said, sitting back in his chair and steepling his fingers.

"Actually, we've hit a considerable snag," Valentina told him. "The electrician I fired last week was worse than we thought. All the previous timelines he gave us are way off. It's going to take Tanner weeks longer on every job."

"What about the ones that are already done?" Radcliffe asked, sitting up straight, worry etching a familiar line on his forehead.

"I already looked into it," she told him, glad she kept detailed records so that she had been able to quickly sort her database by contractor before this meeting. "None of the properties the last electrician worked on have been sold yet. He was only with us for about a month."

"Good," Radcliffe said, sitting back again. "Then this is a disappointing development, but not a dangerous one."

"True," she allowed. "None of the families you sold homes to are in any danger. But this puts the project even further in the red."

Radcliffe nodded and then shrugged.

"You know," she said carefully, broaching the real subject she had hoped they could discuss today, "I've been doing some thinking about all that land you have along the proposed highway site."

"Is that so?" Radcliffe asked.

"That land will be a really tough sell as residential lots," she said. "People know the project is coming right through there, and no one wants to build their dream house on top of a highway."

"I'm willing to let that land go cheaply," he said. "With full disclosure about the highway."

"Can we at least *think* about allowing something

commercial to go there?" she asked. "You could limit what kind of businesses would be allowed."

"No," he said simply. "Absolutely not. That's exactly what I was trying to avoid when I came out here and started buying up land. I don't want this town taken over by businesses."

"I understand," she said right away. "I just worry about anyone wanting to build at all, when you're selling houses with new roofing, heaters, and updated electrical wiring in nice locations, all for a song."

"It's all part of the plan," he said. "That land can't be taken by eminent domain if the properties are in good condition."

"But those prices…" she began.

"I'm trying to get the real estate market in Trinity Falls back to where it was before I started overpaying to buy everything up," he told her. "The prices I'm selling for are fair, maybe just a little more than fair for the condition, but I'm happy if local folks can afford them."

She nodded, knowing when she was beaten.

"I knew when I started this that it was going to hurt," he told her with a gentle smile. "But you know I'm a billionaire, right, Valentina?"

She nodded, biting her lip.

Sebastian Radcliffe had never said the word *billionaire* to her before. She got the sense that in some ways the idea of his wealth made him uncomfortable. And since he had grown up modestly like she had, she understood it.

"So even if this winds up a net loss, I didn't have to borrow to do it, and I've got other investments that will turn out better," he went on. "Your job isn't in danger. My family won't starve, and we won't lose our home. If the Trinity Falls project winds up deep in the red then I'll live a little more carefully for a while, or even forever, and I'll still be happy—so long as this town doesn't lose itself. That's all I ever wanted."

It was a beautiful thing to say, and truly a wonderful thing he had done here. The more she got to know the town, the more Valentina understood why Radcliffe had been desperate to save it from commercial developers.

It was just a shame that Trinity Falls was the first major project he'd put her in charge of. She certainly wasn't going to be able to move into a higher position in the city if her first big deal wound up costing the investor most of his fortune.

"Hey, Baz," Emma's voice sang out from the doorway. She always called her fiancé by the shortened version of his first name. "Hi, Valentina."

"Hi, Emma," Valentina said, feeling genuinely glad to see her friend. "What are you up to today?"

"I'm here to steal Baz to taste the test cake," Emma said, eyebrows waggling. "Can I steal you too? The more testers, the merrier."

"Oh, I've got a full docket today," Valentina said. "But thank you."

"Ugh, you're all work and no play," Emma teased. "But I'll catch up with you later. Natalie's up to something, and I know I'll get it out of you."

"I don't know what you're talking about," Valentina said, smoothing down her skirt in a classic business school move that indicated the conversation was over, and didn't let your negotiating opponent look you in the eye to see that you had something to hide. "But let's sneak off for a coffee later, if you have time."

"Sure," Emma said. "Baz will be getting Wes off the bus for *guy time* at three-thirty."

"Don't say it like that," Radcliffe said indulgently. "Guy time is important."

Valentina wondered if there was another businessman alive as powerful as Sebastian Radcliffe who personally picked up their son from the bus every day and had a snack with him.

She was truly happy to see the two of them bonding more. Wes had gone from being taken to and from an elite private school by a chauffeur each day, to piling on and off a country school bus full of rowdy kids, and she had never seen him happier.

And the way Emma smiled up at her fiancé told Valentina she was only teasing about *guy time*. She clearly loved both Radcliffe men with all her heart. And Valentina couldn't be more pleased for her boss and his son.

But for some reason she couldn't put her finger on, all their love and happiness left her with an unexpected feeling of longing in her chest today.

5

TANNER

That afternoon, Tanner stood outside the elementary school, taking in the sight of all the bundled-up parents and little brothers and sisters waiting for pickup. A row of yellow school buses formed a line on the side of the building and the air was filled with tiny snow flurries and anticipation.

Though he'd had more than enough to do today, Tanner finished his first round of checks on the houses rewired by Linck early enough to pick up his son at school. He figured they could walk into town and enjoy the hint of snow coming down, and Tanner could hear about Zeke's school day instead of just what happened on the bus.

The bell rang inside and a little girl standing with her mom started jumping up and down excitedly.

"That means Leah's coming," the girl squeaked.

"She sure is," her mother said with a smile.

The other parents in earshot all smiled at each other,

and even though they were mostly moms and grandmas, Tanner got smiled at too.

People were getting used to seeing him around. When he'd been a single dad at the community play group back when Zeke was tiny, it had been a little different. It felt like the moms viewed him with a certain amount of suspicion at first. By now, he was just part of the scenery.

Kids began pouring out the front doors of the school, and Tanner started getting excited himself. He remembered heading out of this very school when he was small, filled with joy at knowing that he was going back to the homestead to run and play with his cousins, and eat warm cookies or whatever other delicious snack the grown-ups had waiting for them.

"*Daddy*," Zeke yelled when he spotted him.

Tanner watched as his seven-year-old son sprinted in his direction, his backpack thudding against his back so hard that Tanner was afraid the child would be tipped over by it if it picked up any more momentum.

Tanner bent to hug him as he zoomed in.

"No bus today?" Zeke panted as he flung himself into his father's arms.

"Nope," Tanner told him. "I left my truck in town because I was thinking maybe you'd want to walk through the snow flurries with me and get our snack at the bakery."

"*Yes,*" Zeke yelled in delight.

"Let's do it," Tanner said, straightening up. "Want me to carry your backpack?"

"Okay," Zeke told him, shouldering it off and holding it up.

Though it looked enormous on the boy, it actually wasn't all that heavy. Tanner just hoped there wasn't too much homework in it.

"Can we build a snowman tonight?" Zeke asked as they headed for the footpath to the village.

"I'm not sure about that," Tanner told him, trying not to chuckle. "We aren't supposed to get much more snow than this. It's pretty, but it won't stick to the ground."

"Oh," Zeke said a little sadly.

"But that makes it nice to walk in," Tanner told him. "It looks like a snow globe, but we won't slip and fall down."

That earned him a big laugh from Zeke.

"I don't fall down in the snow, Dad," he chuckled.

"Well, if you ever do, at least you'll have a nice soft, cold landing," Tanner offered.

Zeke melted into more giggles and for a minute Tanner got to feel like a stand-up comedian.

"How were your friends today?" Tanner asked. "Did anyone get kicked out of school?"

"*No,*" Zeke laughed. "No, Daddy, they were all really good."

"Are you sure?" Tanner asked, pretending to be suspicious. "Not even that naughty Ezekiel Williams?"

"That's *me,* Dad," Zeke shrieked in delight, laughing so hard he actually did melt onto the ground for a minute, like a snowman in the sunshine. "*I'm* Ezekiel Williams."

"Oh, right," Tanner said, nodding wisely. "That name did sound familiar."

"Why are you so silly today?" Zeke asked, using Tanner's leg to pull himself back up.

Tanner had asked Zeke the same thing so many times that he was broadsided by a terrible pang of sentimentality.

Don't grow up too fast, buddy...

"Dad?" Zeke said.

"I had a good day, I guess," he told the boy, as they continued their walk.

"That's nice," Zeke said. "Why was it good?"

Tanner wasn't really sure, but when he thought back all he could see was Valentina's eyes widening when she realized she had leaned on the paint, and then the sparkling wonderland at the electric supply shop that reminded him of her earrings.

"I made a new friend," he realized out loud.

"What's his name?" Zeke asked.

"*Her* name is Valentina," Tanner told him.

"Is she going to be my stepmom?" Zeke asked casually.

Tanner was so surprised that he looked down at Zeke, and tripped over a tree root that lifted the sidewalk slightly, barely catching his balance before he dropped Zeke's backpack.

"No," Tanner said. "No. What would make you think that?"

"Uncle Ansel got married and now Lucas has a stepmom," Zeke said shrugging. "She makes art projects with him. And he has a stepsister now, too. Does Vallerina have a daughter?"

"Valentina," Tanner corrected him automatically. "And no, she doesn't have any kids. I don't think."

Come to think of it, he didn't know much about her at all, except that she was loyal and wore pretty earrings. And she had listened to him today like she cared about what he was saying.

"You should definitely ask her if she has any kids before you marry her," Zeke suggested wisely. "We have to be sure we have enough space for everyone when they move in."

"I'm not marrying her," Tanner said, stopping in his tracks and wondering how they had gotten this far in the conversation without him making that clear. "We just work together."

"Oh," Zeke said, looking mildly disappointed again. "Can we get brownies with ice cream on top?"

"Uh, sure," Tanner said, shaking his head at Zeke's seven-year-old change of topic.

"*Yes,*" Zeke exclaimed for the second time in two minutes.

Tanner was surprised to hear Zeke talk in such a positive way about stepmoms, although he guessed he really shouldn't be. Winona and Parker had been a huge boon to his cousin Ansel's life. Ansel and Lucas were definitely a lot happier these days, and that was likely why Zeke had taken an interest.

Tanner had never really considered dating again, but it was interesting to think Zeke wouldn't have a problem with it if he did. Though he'd have to have a talk with the boy about how it all worked before he scared off some poor woman by asking her to pick out curtains or something.

Then he thought about the demands of his work, and the attention Zeke needed, and he knew he wasn't really going to date, at least not until Zeke was grown up and he didn't have to weigh every job against whether it would interfere with being the boy's sole parent.

"*Christmas*," Zeke yelled, spotting the candy canes hanging from the lampposts.

"Not too much longer," Tanner agreed. "It's right around the corner."

"I want to get Mrs. Hastings something with a bear on it," Zeke reminded him for the tenth time. "She loves bears."

No matter how much Mrs. Hastings tortured Zeke with her endless homework drills, Zeke still adored her. He had been so excited to shop for her Christmas present that he barely mentioned what he wanted for himself.

"We'll find something great," Tanner promised the boy.

Hopefully, they could find it in the shop at Cassidy Farm or one of the stores in town. The mall up on Route One had everything, but Tanner preferred supporting his neighbors when he could. After all, he was grateful when they hired him instead of going to the big shop out in Springton Valley. For Tanner, loyalty went both ways.

Zeke jogged backwards to take his father's hand as they crossed the street from Columbia Avenue over to Park, and Tanner was reminded yet again of what a great kid he had. At Zeke's age, his mother definitely had to yell at him about holding hands to cross the street.

"Let's check the house," Zeke squeaked when they got to the other side, tugging Tanner over to the window of the real estate office.

A beautiful dollhouse that resembled some of the Victorian homes in Trinity Falls was displayed in the window year-round, but during the holiday season, it was carefully decorated, bit by bit. The house had been sitting in a bed of soft cotton snow since the day after Thanksgiving, and tiny lights had appeared on it last week. The latest addition appeared to be a tiny, decorated Christmas tree in one of the windows. A miniature Santa Claus would appear in the chimney just before the holiday, an event Tanner remembered being excited about when he was a kid himself.

Zeke pressed his little nose against the glass and Tanner almost pulled him back, until he saw Sloane Greenfield smiling at them from her desk on the other side of the window. Probably a lot of kids were smashing their faces against that glass at this time of year. He gave her a quick wave and, then a voice from the doorway of the shop next door called out to them.

"If it isn't my best customers," Mallory, the owner of the bakery chimed, holding a plastic bowl in her hand.

"Is that for dogs?" Zeke asked, excitedly peeling himself off the window and turning his attention to Mallory.

"It sure is," she told him. "I just put fresh water in it. Do you want to set it in front of the shop for me? It needs to go in a spot where no one will trip over it."

"Sure," Zeke said, running over to her looking delighted that she had asked for his help.

"Just be careful," she told him. "You wouldn't want to get covered in water when it's so cold out."

He took the bowl as carefully as if it was filled with eggs, and lowered it to the ideal spot—exactly where Mallory always put it.

"Wow," she said. "Thank you so much, Zeke. That's just perfect."

"You're welcome," he said proudly, glancing over at his dad as if to make sure he'd seen.

"Zeke's a great helper," he told Mallory. "He even has chores at home now, and it makes things so much easier for me."

"Oh, yeah?" Mallory asked.

"I set the table," Zeke told her. "And I help wash dishes."

"Oh, I could put you right to work here," Mallory said, frowning and pretending to think up jobs. "If you came here looking for a job to do, you're in the right place."

"I came for a snack," Zeke said thoughtfully. "But I can probably help you until it's time to do my homework."

Tanner felt a pang of pride at his son's selflessness.

"I'm only teasing," Mallory said, bending down to tousle his hair. "But you're a great kid, and if you still want to work for me when you grow up, you can come see me anytime."

"Okay," Zeke said happily.

Mallory smiled at Tanner over Zeke's head, giving him the same smile he saw so often when people were charmed by his son. He let her know what they were having—a zucchini muffin for him, a small brownie with ice cream for Zeke, and two hot chocolates.

Zeke was already settling in at their favorite table—one at the back so he could watch Mallory use the cool, old-fashioned cash register that actually made a *ding* sound whenever she opened the drawer.

"I wish we could make a snowman," Zeke said suddenly, his eyes on the delicate flurries falling on the village out the big front windows of the bakery.

"Well, we won't be able to do that, but maybe we can fix the snowman decoration we got from Big Jim," Tanner offered.

Tanner owned an apartment building in town that had a nice garden to one side. He had started putting out Christmas decorations a few years ago, and before long, what had been a fun little display had become something everyone in town waited for. People even started donating decorations that no longer worked. Which was perfect, since he was an electrician, and it was usually a snap to refurbish old ones and get them lit up again.

"Yes," Zeke said. "I want to do that."

"Let's just have a look at your homework first," Tanner said. "You know we normally only work on the lights on weekends."

Zeke industriously dug into his backpack and fished out a list, a notebook, and a workbook.

Tanner took the list and scanned it. The reading homework was just to read for ten minutes before bed, which was easy since they did more than that most nights anyway. But there were also a bunch of pages in the workbook that had to be completed, along with a handwritten page of sums in Zeke's notebook.

It was too much.

But Tanner knew he couldn't get angry or complain openly in front of the boy. It was important for Zeke to understand that his teacher was an authority figure, and that authority figures needed to be treated with respect.

Besides, Zeke loved Mrs. Hastings. He wouldn't want to hear anything negative about her.

He'll just think he's having a hard time finishing the work because he's not good at math...

That kind of thinking could close off doors in the boy's mind that were open right now.

"I'm sorry, buddy," he said, feeling a lump in his own throat. "I think we'll just have our nice snack and head home to get to work. We probably have some tricky math problems to solve today."

He'd done his best to put a positive spin on things, but the look in Zeke's eyes nearly broke his heart.

6

TANNER

A few days later Tanner pulled up his truck past the *Whispering Ridge* sign and into Radcliffe's gravel lot, his stomach already twisting in knots.

He'd been really looking forward to this meeting with Valentina, and he'd done a ton of prep for it. The only thing he hadn't done was make sure that Zeke would be in school. Unfortunately, today was one of the seemingly random teacher in-service days that always managed to take him by surprise.

"Okay, Zeke," he said as brightly as he could. "You know the drill, right?"

"I'll sit quietly and work on my homework," Zeke said right away. "I won't interrupt, and I won't touch anything."

"Exactly," Tanner said, relieved. "When we're done, if you were good, we'll go wherever you want for the afternoon."

"Okay," Zeke said. "But how long will it take?"

It wasn't the first time he had asked, and it was making Tanner nervous. He didn't expect his son to have to cope with the adult world very often. Normally, he got a sitter if anything he had to do interfered with time when Zeke wasn't at school. Today had just snuck up on him somehow. They waited alone on the corner for a bus that never came, and he finally checked the school calendar on the fridge only to realize his mistake.

He probably should have brought toys and games for Zeke. The boy was used to having his dad by his side, at least for moral support, while he did his math. And of course Tanner hadn't even told Valentina that he was bringing his son.

This won't be a disaster, he tried to tell himself as they got out of the car. *Zeke is charming. She'll love him.*

But try as he might, he couldn't exactly picture Valentina giggling at Zeke's lighthearted proclamations and joking around with him like the other young women in town. She seemed so serious, and so devoted to her work.

What if she thinks a single dad is the wrong person for the job?

He had other work. Tanner always managed to stay busy and keep a roof over their heads. But this big project for Baz was a real blessing, and a chance to get ahead.

If she doesn't fire me for showing up with my son...

"Wow, horses," Zeke said happily, pointing to the big field beyond the farmhouse.

Sure enough, there were horses out there between the house and the wooded ridge. A breeze kicked up, and the murmuring sound of the wind through those trees reminded Tanner how Whispering Ridge got its name.

"Hi there," Valentina called out from the front porch of the big house.

"Hi," Zeke yelled before Tanner had a chance to respond. "I like your earrings. They look like fireworks."

"Thank you," she replied. "I'm Valentina."

"I'm Zeke," he said politely.

He sprinted up the steps a little faster than Tanner would have liked and stuck his hand out.

Tanner held his breath.

But Valentina merely smiled and shook Zeke's hand, like having a meeting with a second grader was an everyday occurrence.

"Hi, Miss Jimenez," Tanner said, jogging up the steps to join them.

"Valentina," she corrected him. A half-smile seemed to lurk somewhere in her eyes.

"Valentina," he echoed, inwardly begging himself to tear his gaze from hers so he could remember what he came here for. "I forgot the school had an in-service today. Zeke brought some homework with him, if that's okay."

"That's fine," she said. "I have a nice big table in my office, and I might have something more fun to do than homework. Do you like mazes, Zeke?"

Zeke ran up to follow her into the house, the two of them calmly discussing what kind of maze she meant. She spoke to Zeke like he was a tiny adult, and he was clearly delighted to rise to the occasion.

"I meant a paper maze," she was saying as they entered her office. "But a corn maze does sound like fun."

"They have one at Cassidy Farm," Zeke told her. "I can solve it."

"That sounds really neat," she said. "But I would probably be worried about getting lost in a cornfield myself."

"You should go through with someone else the first time," Zeke told her sensibly, repeating exactly what Tanner had told him on their first visit to the maze. "I can take you through, if you want."

"Thank you for that offer, Zeke," she said, pulling a book out of her desk drawer along with a box of crayons. "This is a maze book you might like. Some of the mazes are already done, but most of them are still waiting for someone clever enough to solve them."

Zeke grabbed the book and crayons right out of her hands and hustled over to the table, curling himself over the book immediately, then popping his head up.

"Thank you," he said, before Tanner had to remind him.

"You're very welcome," she replied.

It was funny how Zeke reacted to Valentina's calm, respectful way with him. Tanner had never really seen his son match someone else's mood the way he was doing right now.

"Shall we get started?" she asked, turning to Tanner.

"Yes, sure," he said, scrambling over to take a seat across from her at the desk. "I've got time estimates worked out on my tablet. Baz let me know that materials aren't an issue as far as budget. Is that right?"

"We don't cut corners," Valentina agreed, with an expression that spoke of her total agreement with her boss.

Baz might have been the one who said, *Money is no object, just do it right.* But it was clearly Valentina who was on the ground day to day making sure that philosophy was put into action.

Tanner opened up the program he used for time estimates and started with the first house.

"There are seven houses in the valley," Valentina said, frowning. "Is this the correct order you're proposing?"

"I know it's sort of in the middle of the others," Tanner said. "But I talked with some of the crews, and I think this one is probably the closest to being done, other than electrical. I can work in any order you want, but I thought it might be good to try and get the first few of these up and running a little faster."

"You already spoke with the other crews?" she asked.

"I mean, I know a lot of the HVAC guys anyway," he said, worrying that maybe he had overstepped. "They call me all the time on their other jobs to upgrade service panels and put in subs when people retrofit for Central Air, so I just swung over there..."

"I think it's great," she told him, placing her hand on the edge of his tablet, as if to stop him from making excuses. "I really appreciate you taking the initiative like that."

"I was glad to," he told her. "I respect that you're the boss though, Miss—I mean, Valentina."

"Thank you," she said.

This time, the smile hiding in her eyes made its way

to her face and he was stunned to see that his very serious boss had *dimples*.

"So," she went on. "What else is on here?"

They turned their attention back to his tablet. He was glad he had taken the time to put together a sort of presentation that was easier for her to follow than his usual chicken scratch on a clipboard.

Valentina took notes, stopping him to ask a question here or there. But he relaxed after a few minutes when it became clear that she wasn't looking for reasons to pick his plan apart.

"What's this?" she asked, looking at an afternoon block he had scheduled back at a previous job.

"If the paint crew is done with the patches and touch-up after the knob and tube, I'll come back to install the hardwired smoke alarms then," he told her. "That way they won't get paint on them. They make plastic caps, but I'd rather not risk it."

"Wow," she said, looking both pleased and relieved.

"So, I think we can get caught up in about six weeks, if we stick to this plan," he told her. "But unexpected things always come up, and we want everything done right. So maybe you'd better tell Baz eight weeks, and we can surprise him for the best if it all goes smoothly."

"That's why he said you'd take your time," she said softly.

"Who said that?" Tanner asked, feeling a little prickled that Baz would say it when they'd never worked together.

"Randy," she said, looking a little embarrassed. "I'm not sure if he meant for me to repeat it. I thought he meant you were a slow worker, which honestly had me a little worried. But now I can see he meant you would take the time you needed to get the job done right."

"Huh," Tanner said, leaning back and nodding. "I mean, I guess he would be the one who knows how long everyone takes on these things, since he opens the permits and closes them out afterward."

"I think you should take it as a compliment," she said. "Mr. Radcliffe will certainly see it that way. I'll make sure he knows how much work you've put into this plan."

"Thank you," Tanner said, suddenly remembering this was an important work meeting. For a few minutes there, it had felt like a fun way to show off something he had grown good at over many years of practice to someone who was actually in a position to appreciate it.

"Oh," she said. "Speaking of Randy, he did me a *huge* favor."

"Yeah?" Tanner asked, leaning in again.

"He said if I want to text him photos of some of the work, he can look over them before the inspection dates," she said, her eyes sparkling. "That way if he's going to want a change, we can get it done before he comes out. It could save a ton of time scheduling re-inspections."

"It sure could," Tanner said, amazed. "How on earth did you get him to agree to that?"

"I didn't even ask," Valentina said. "He offered after I brought over breakfast."

"You made him breakfast?" Tanner asked, delighted at how brilliant that was. Randy seemed to work from sunrise to sunset on the days he was on duty. It was only natural for him to be pleased with a nice meal.

"I can't really take credit," she said, waving her hand. "I just picked up his favorite at *Jolly Beans.*"

"I'm hungry," Zeke said suddenly, his first addition to the conversation, most likely inspired by the mere mention of food.

"Well, that's perfect," Valentina said. "Because I did actually bake these myself."

She opened another desk drawer and pulled out a small, plastic-wrap covered plate of pastries.

"Empanadas," she told them, placing the little plate on the table with a flourish. "They're my grandmother's recipe."

"Wow," Zeke said happily, half climbing over the table to grab one. "Thank you."

"You're ready for anything," Tanner said to her, impressed.

"Spoken like a man who understands the value of preparation," she said, arching a brow at the plan open on his tablet. "Eat up. I'm just going to send Mr. Radcliffe a quick reminder."

"These are *good*," Zeke said with his mouth full. "They're full of stew."

"Finish chewing," Tanner told him before taking a bite himself.

The flaky empanada melted in his mouth like butter, and the savory flavor of chicken burst on his tongue.

"Oh, wow," he said with his own mouth full.

Valentina smiled again, though she kept her eyes on her computer monitor as she typed out a message.

And once again, Tanner couldn't help noticing her dimples. She had another pair of long, dangly earrings on today, and the late morning sun coming in the window by her desk lit them up, sending diamonds of light dancing on the walls when she moved her head.

Magical, a little voice in the back of his head whispered, and he realized that he might be falling for her, just a little bit.

But he couldn't afford to think like that. He was already overwhelmed with work and fatherhood. And besides, he was reporting to her on the biggest project he'd ever undertaken.

If I start something with her and things go wrong, I don't want my chances here to be—

"Finished," Zeke yelled.

"That was a good empanada, huh?" Tanner asked, shaking off his worries.

"Yes," Zeke said. "But I already ate that. I finished my *maze.*"

"No way," Valentina said, looking up at him.

"Yes," Zeke said, practically dancing in his chair. "See."

He held up the book, but Valentina got up and came over, pulling out the chair beside him.

"Wow," she said, seating herself. "You really did. And you know what's even more impressive?"

"What?" Zeke asked.

"You did it in one try," she said.

Tanner glanced over and saw that she was right. Zeke's blue crayon line led from the entrance of the maze right to the center, without any mistakes.

"What do you mean?" Zeke asked.

"Here," Valentina said, paging through the book.

"Here's one that another child did, when he was a little older than you."

The other child had to be Wes Radcliffe, who was eleven now, and plenty smart. Tanner frowned at the many loop backs and attempts that came before success.

"Yours is really amazing, isn't it?" Valentina asked, turning back to the page Zeke had worked on. "How did you do it?"

"I looked at it," Zeke said. "And I thought about it first."

"So you sort of followed the path in your mind," Valentina said. "Before you started tracing it?"

"Yes," Zeke said, nodding. "That's what I did."

"Did you know that you're super smart?" Valentina asked him, without a hint of condescension in her voice. "Most adults I know couldn't do that."

Zeke glanced over at Tanner, hope flickering in his eyes.

Tanner smiled at him and nodded, confirming what Valentina had said, even as his heart broke at the idea that his son had ever felt anything but smart and capable.

"Wow," Zeke said. "But... I always take too long with my math homework."

Tanner longed to jump in and explain that the teacher was overwhelming the kids with so much drilling that probably every child took too long.

"That's a different kind of smart," Valentina said dismissively. "Being quick at math problems won't be important when you grow up. You'll just use a calculator, like everyone else. But being patient enough to solve a maze, and visualizing and memorizing a path without tracing it? That's really cool, Zeke. Maybe one day you'll be an air traffic controller, or maybe you'll work for NASA."

Zeke rose out of his chair as if he had been lifted by an unseen hand, and the next thing Tanner knew, the boy was wrapping himself around Valentina in a giant bear hug.

Tanner was pretty sure Zeke's hands were still sticky from the empanada, and even if they weren't, he'd been playing outside all morning, which showed in the not-so-clean clothes that were currently wrapped around Valentina's pristine white blouse and gray trousers.

But before Tanner could open his mouth, Valentina hugged Zeke back.

"That's the best hug I've had in a long time," she said warmly when she pulled back.

"Thank you," Zeke said, looking up at her. "Except my dad gives the *best* hugs."

"Oh yeah?" she asked him, her eyes dancing.

"He gives big bear hugs," Zeke said, nodding with a serious look on his face.

Big bear hugs and little bear hugs had been kind of a thing with them since Zeke was tiny. Tanner was moved that the boy still talked about hugging his dad without embarrassment. He knew that wouldn't last forever.

"I'll keep that in mind," Valentina told him. "In case I ever need a big bear hug. And I'm glad you liked the empanadas."

"We have a present for you too," Zeke said.

"Just a work thing," Tanner said quickly. "It's nothing, really."

"Oh," she said, turning to him.

He pulled out the paper bag that held the coverall and handed it to her quickly, hoping she didn't think it was stupid. She took it out of the bag, her brow furrowed at the purple fabric until she unfolded it.

He held his breath as she looked it over.

"Oh my goodness," Valentina said, her eyes lighting up. "This is amazing."

"It's just for when you visit on site," he said quickly. "So you don't get any more paint on your pretty clothes."

"And it's purple," Zeke pointed out.

"My favorite color," Valentina told him with a big smile.

Valentina's phone buzzed on her desk, and she glanced over worriedly.

"We've taken up most of your morning," Tanner said right away. "Thank you for hearing me out, and for the treats, and for letting Zeke borrow your maze book."

"He's welcome back to do another one anytime," she said, flashing both of them a smile as she headed over to her desk for her phone. "Thank you so much for my coverall. Good luck with your math, Zeke, and I'll see you in the valley, Tanner."

"Definitely," he told her.

Zeke grabbed his backpack full of homework and they headed out together.

"She said I was smart," he whispered loudly as soon as they were two steps out of her office. "And she liked her present."

Tanner glanced back, pretty certain Valentina had heard that.

Sure enough, her dimples were showing, even though she was talking business on the phone.

She really likes him, he couldn't help thinking.

Something in his chest seemed to settle into place, and he felt more relaxed without really knowing why.

7

VALENTINA

Later that night, Valentina stood in Natalie Cassidy's kitchen, watching Natalie pour mugs of hot apple cider from the urn on the counter.

Tonight was supposed to be a dress fitting for all the bridesmaids in Emma's wedding. But it was clear that trying on dresses was the last thing on anyone's mind.

Instead, they were all laughing and chatting about work and family, and all the things going on in town for the holiday. It seemed like everyone had a pet project or a favorite gathering this time of year.

Emma was there with them, looking relaxed and happy in spite of how quickly her wedding was coming up.

She's marrying a kind man who adores her, Valentina reminded herself. From all she knew about Emma, Valentina guessed that she probably didn't care about little things at the wedding ceremony not being perfect, because she was just so happy that she was going to be

Sebastian Radcliffe's wife and Wes's stepmom at the end of it.

Melody Davis was another person at the gathering that Valentina already knew a little bit through Emma. Melody was on the quiet side, but Valentina could tell right away why Emma had been friends with her since high school, and why she had chosen her as a bridesmaid. Melody was good-natured and had a surprisingly great sense of humor for someone so introverted.

Tonight, it was clear that Melody was more comfortable when she was among her inner circle. She was laughing like a hyena at a funny story Natalie had shared about her daughter, Rumor, who was now in kindergarten. Valentina felt a moment of gratitude to be included with all of these wonder women.

"Well, at least they know now to tell the kids they have to let the paint dry first," Natalie finished, smiling as her friends laughed.

Natalie adored Rumor and Wyatt, her husband Shane's kids. It was easy to forget that she was a stepmom, like Emma would soon be.

Maybe that's what it would be like to be Zeke's stepmom, she found herself thinking unexpectedly.

Wild ideas like that one had been popping into her head ever since their meeting this morning. She knew she should be ashamed of herself. Poor Tanner Williams was just trying to work on a project, and for some reason she was weaving fairy tales for herself about him and his adorable son.

"What are you thinking about?" Emma asked.

Valentina looked up and realized Emma was talking to her.

"Oh, just work stuff," she said, wondering how silly she looked.

"Didn't you have a meeting with Tanner Williams this morning?" Emma asked. "Baz said you really liked him."

"He's a smart guy," Valentina said a little too quickly. "That's all. I just liked his plans."

She didn't realize how defensive she was being until the others went silent, letting her words hang in the air an extra moment.

Natalie and Melody exchanged a glance, and Emma just nodded at Valentina, looking like she was going to erupt in giggles any second.

"Hello," Alice Cassidy's voice came from the center hall. *"I brought over a few things. I could use a hand, sweetheart."*

Valentina thanked her lucky stars as everyone's attention turned to Natalie's mother-in-law's arrival.

"He's really nice," Melody said softly as the others headed down the hallway to greet Alice and help with whatever she had brought. "Not to say that you're interested, but if you were, you could do a whole lot worse than Tanner Williams."

"Is that so?" Valentina said lightly.

She wanted nothing more than to pin Melody to the wall and interrogate her. After all, Melody had grown up in Trinity Falls, and that meant she had known Tanner since they were all kids. But Valentina had to at least pretend to be an adult and not some lovesick teenager with a crush.

"He thinks things through," Melody said thoughtfully. "He always has. And he hasn't dated since his divorce, even though it was forever ago. He puts his little boy first. So if he likes you, it really means something."

"Well, he doesn't like me," Valentina said, feeling a little down about it, but glad Melody had been honest with her. "We had a nice meeting today, and Zeke was with him. I kind of hit it off with Zeke is all."

"Well, that might just be the way to his heart," Melody said with a half-smile. "Who knows?"

"Here we go," Alice said happily as she came into the kitchen, a cloud of pretty, emerald-green dresses in her arms. "I've got my sewing basket on the porch, so if anything needs any taking in or letting out, we're all set."

"And she brought so much food," Natalie called from the hallway.

"Just some gingerbread and a little supper," Alice said. "Dining room table okay for the dresses, dear?"

"Yes, thank you," Natalie told her as she came in, holding a cardboard box with a slow cooker crock in it. "And if there's corned beef and cabbage in here, I'm going to cry with joy."

"Grab your tissues then," Alice said, laughing.

"If you feed us too much, you'll need to let out all the dresses," Melody teased.

"You'll be eating well at the wedding too," Alice said briskly. "We want these dresses built with room for feasting."

"I think I love everything about your wedding, Emma," Valentina decided out loud, wrapping an arm around her new friend's shoulders.

"If a good meal makes you feel that way, then you were made for this town," Emma said, laughing. "Come on, everyone, let's try on these dresses. I want to see all my princesses looking the part."

Valentina tried to hide her smile at the thought that Emma had no idea how much they would look like princesses when they rode up on horseback. But that idea also made her nervous, since she still had to find time to learn how to ride.

The trouble was that the only two places to learn to ride in town were the Williams Estate, where Emma was the instructor, and Cassidy Farm. But Valentina had already told Natalie Cassidy that she could ride.

I'm not going to worry about it today, she told herself.

After all, she had made her way through Wharton and been hired by Sebastian Radcliffe. Surely she could do what every ten-year old child in summer camp did and sit on the back of a horse for a few minutes.

"Oh, wow," Natalie sighed appreciatively, holding up her dress for everyone to see.

It was clear that Emma wasn't one of those brides who wanted to outshine her bridesmaids. The beautiful emerald-green gown was nearly identical to the ones Valentina and the others would wear, with an embroidered bodice and a skirt that flowed down in what looked like miles of ballerina tulle.

Alice Cassidy smiled over the crew of girls as they all exclaimed over the dresses. Her chestnut brown hair with the streaks of gray was pulled back in a bun, and she wore a simple red dress with a pretty apron on top. The whole house was starting to smell heavenly from the crock she had brought.

Even though it was different in so many ways, something about the situation felt like home to Valentina, and she was momentarily frozen, soaking it in as she remembered family get-togethers with her parents and grandmother, neighbors stopping by with their favorite dishes, and everyone talking and laughing together.

Belatedly, she realized Alice was observing her with a furrow in her brow. She had been caught daydreaming twice in one evening.

"Did you really make these dresses yourself?" Valentina asked her. "They're so beautiful."

"Thank you," Alice said, beaming. "I loved every minute of it. My grandchildren mostly like store-bought clothing these days, so when I whip things up for them, they have to be simple. It was a pleasure to make something so fanciful for a change."

"I can't wait to try mine on," Valentina told her.

A few minutes later, she was in a guest room up on the third floor of the house, looking at herself in the mirror.

The pretty bodice fit perfectly, and she couldn't help spinning around and watching the tulle lift and swirl with her, feeling a bit like a little girl playing dress-up.

When she stopped spinning and spotted the smile on her face, she couldn't help feeling that the whole dress design had been made just for her.

Maybe one day Alice Cassidy could make my wedding gown...

That thought had come unbidden, and she shook her

head at her own nonsense before putting her regular clothes back on and heading into the hallway.

She was the first bridesmaid down the stairs. But before she could make it into the dining room to thank Alice and let her know it was a perfect fit, she bumped into Emma in the center hall. She had a gingerbread man in one hand, and she grabbed Valentina by the elbow with the other.

"What's up?" Valentina whispered, as Emma dragged her into the front parlor, where Shane and Natalie's Christmas tree twinkled with pretty lights that illuminated the kids' many homemade ornaments.

"I know I kind of put you on the spot earlier about my cousin Tanner," Emma said quietly. "I really did just mean to ask you about work, but I can't stop thinking about you and him now."

Me neither, Valentina thought to herself.

"I actually think you two could be perfect together," Emma went on, keeping her voice low enough Valentina didn't worry about them being overheard. "I'm not saying it to pressure you, and I get that he already has a kid and that means... well, it complicates things. Anyway, I just wanted to let you know that I've obviously known him all my life and he's a great guy—steady, kind, and *fun*. You could be good for each other."

"Oh, wow," Valentina said, feeling flustered. Suddenly, all she wanted was to admit her feelings to Emma.

But the truth was that it would be terrible to get tangled up over a guy when she was so close to achieving all her career goals. Her father had given up so much to give her this chance...

"It means the world to me that you think I have something to offer your cousin," she said carefully. "But I'm so busy with work. I know you understand, since you're engaged to Mr. Radcliffe."

"Why don't you ever call him Baz?" Emma demanded. "I know he's asked you to."

Valentina bit her lip and tried to come up with an answer.

"I'm not sure," she admitted after a moment. "But I want to be respectful. I want us both to remember what our purpose is here. Just because we're out in the fresh air, and he's chopping wood and going on hikes, doesn't mean I can get lazy when it comes to doing everything I can to safeguard his investments."

"Oh, Valentina," Emma said, her face falling. "Baz knows that. You're the most loyal person in the world. But you're also like family to us. You know that, right?"

Like family to us was a phrase Valentina had heard before in her life. Unfortunately, it hadn't carried much weight in the long run. But she smiled and gave Emma a quick hug, knowing that her friend meant what she said.

"Thank you," she told her. "I'll think about it."

"Think about Tanner, too," Emma whispered in her ear as she hugged her close.

Valentina nodded, and she knew she would. But she also knew she wouldn't let herself do anything more than that.

After all, she had worked her whole life to leave her mark on the world and make her parents' sacrifices worthwhile. She couldn't just let herself get stuck in the first little town where she found someone she liked.

"*Dinner,*" Natalie called out as she came down the stairs.

"I guess that's our cue," Emma said, letting go of Valentina. "Hey, you know Caroline and Winona couldn't make it tonight. I'm seeing Winona tomorrow. But is there any chance you'd be able to bring Caroline her dress to try on? I wouldn't ask, but I know your place is right across from the library."

"Of course," Valentina told her, happy to finally have Emma ask for something she could enthusiastically agree to. "I'll go over to the library first thing tomorrow."

And by then, all these silly thoughts will be out of my head for good.

8

VALENTINA

Valentina stood in the library bathroom the next morning, listening to the rustle of tulle as Caroline Williams tried on her bridesmaid dress.

"Oh wow," Caroline said from inside the stall. "It fits like a glove."

"Come on out," Valentina said. "Let's see it."

Caroline emerged looking absolutely stunning. She smiled at herself in the mirror and twirled around just like Valentina had back at Natalie's place.

"I'm being silly," Caroline said with an awkward giggle.

"I did *exactly* the same thing when I tried mine on," Valentina assured her. "I don't know how she did it, but Emma managed to choose a color that looks great on everyone. And the fit looks just right too. Alice Cassidy is an amazing seamstress."

"It's perfect," Caroline said with a smile. "But I need to get it off before something happens to it."

"I guess being a children's librarian can be messy," Valentina realized out loud.

"Definitely," Caroline said from back inside the stall. "We had finger painting out on the library lawn last summer. I'm still finding multicolored fingerprints all over the library, and that activity happened *outside*."

"It's really great that you do so much for the kids," Valentina said.

"We want them to get used to coming to the library," Caroline told her. "If they think of this place as fun, they won't hesitate to come back when they're older. And not just to check out books, but also if they need help or information."

"Interesting," Valentina said, suddenly thinking of her impasse with Radcliffe.

"You okay?" Caroline asked after a moment of quiet.

"Well," Valentina said. "What you said about people coming here for help gave me an idea. Do you think that you could help me find some information about the town?"

"Absolutely," Caroline said, coming out of the stall again with her dress over her arm and an eager expression. "What are you looking for?"

"I wanted to know more about the economy of Trinity Falls," Valentina said. "What are the economic challenges here? And what are the strengths? Do you have any economic data like that about the town on file?"

"I don't think so," Caroline said, frowning thoughtfully. "At least not exactly. You might be able to go through the town newspaper archive to get a sense of how things are going."

"Does it have a finance column?" Valentina asked. "That would be terrific."

"Afraid not," Caroline said. "But I'll get you set up with the microfiche, and then I'll ask Helen what else we might have that would help."

"Thanks so much," Valentina said, impressed.

"This is exactly what we're here for," Caroline said. "I only wish we had more of the kind of information you're interested in. I honestly don't think we've ever had this question before."

Caroline looked pleased and frustrated at the same time, and Valentina couldn't help smiling. She understood the mixed feelings of being excited for a challenge, but also frustrated at not being prepared. Clearly, she was in the presence of another woman who was just as obsessed with her work as she was.

AN HOUR LATER, Valentina was still reading back issues of *The Trinity Falls Gazette* on the microfiche machine. And she wasn't really getting anywhere.

All the articles seemed to almost purposefully avoid financial data and instead focused on personal things, like interviews with people who had recently gone on an interesting trip, or listings of which kids had won the bicycle race at the Fourth of July parade.

Between the local sports scores, requests for donations to various charities, and rundowns of movie nights, festivals, and library book clubs, there was basically nothing to indicate which areas of the Trinity Falls business scene were thriving and which were struggling.

Helen stopped over to share the Center for Rural Pennsylvania website and help Valentina navigate it. But the information for Tarker County was limited, and didn't tell her what she really wanted to know.

What do you need? Valentina silently asked Trinity Falls.

The trouble was that the little village and surrounding countryside seemed incredibly self-sufficient, and if there was anything lacking, the people here were definitely prone to keeping a stiff upper lip about it.

Valentina sighed and got up to stretch, realizing that since it was the weekend, she hadn't gotten to enjoy her second cup of coffee with the crews.

That's all I need, she told herself. *I'll run over to Jolly Beans and grab a cup of coffee and then I'll get creative.*

She waved goodbye to Caroline, who was bent over a table with two small children, then grabbed her bag and headed out.

The whole town was ensconced in holiday finery now. Christmas trees were on display on the lawn right outside the library, where volunteers from the fire department were helping families choose which ones to buy. The sweet scent of the pine brought back happy memories of childhood holidays, and Valentina paused, wondering suddenly if she should get a tree for her place.

Don't be silly, she told herself. *It'll just make a mess of pine needles on the floor that I don't have time to clean up. And I can just look out my window at the town tree.*

But it wasn't the same as having her own, and she

knew it. She couldn't help wondering when she would find her place in life and be able to settle down and do things like decorate a Christmas tree.

An image of Tanner Williams lifting Zeke to place the star on a tall Douglas fir flashed through her mind.

Don't, she begged herself.

She was still in her own head, trying to straighten herself out when she found herself face to face with the two main players of her cozy fantasy, as if she had summoned them with her thoughts.

Tanner wore a nice wool coat over a white button-down shirt and jeans, and he was smiling in such a relaxed way as Zeke skipped alongside his dad to keep up with his longer strides. He clutched a stack of books under his right arm.

"Hey," Tanner said, smiling down at Valentina.

"Hi, Valentina," Zeke said. "You went to the library."

"Hi, I sure did," she told him. "I spent a long time there, too."

"But you didn't choose any books," Zeke said sadly, looking at her empty arms.

"I was there to look for information," she said. "So I didn't expect to get any books today."

"Did you find your information?" Tanner asked.

"No," she said, sounding a little sad herself. "I wanted economic data for Trinity Falls. But all I could find were newspapers with articles about parades, pet adoptions, and rained out craft fairs..."

She trailed off, feeling bad about complaining. As Caroline had said, no one had ever asked for the kind of data she was looking for anyway.

"What did you want that kind of info for?" Tanner asked, frowning.

Valentina looked around, and saw they were alone.

"I was hoping I could get Mr. Radcliffe to consider selling some of the land near where the highway is going in for commercial use," she said softly. "It's not selling as residential because no one wants to build a house near the highway. If he was sure that he could sell it for a purpose that served the community, maybe he'd listen to me. There must be businesses this town needs, things that would help Trinity Falls."

"Well, then it sounds like you got exactly the info you needed from the paper," Tanner said.

"What do you mean?" she asked.

"Where are you headed right now?" he asked her instead of answering her question.

"I was just going to grab a coffee," she said.

"Zeke, are you okay with trading in those books in an hour or so?" he asked his son. "I think we should go get breakfast with Miss Jimenez right now."

"Okay," Zeke said happily.

"Come on," Tanner told her. "Let's get some food and get you sorted out."

Valentina couldn't imagine what he had in mind. She was pretty sure Tanner had never done an economic study or a demographics and market analysis.

But there was something about the quiet confidence in his deep voice that made her think maybe he really *was* going to get her sorted out anyway.

9

TANNER

Tanner glanced over at the table by the big window from his spot in line at Jolly Beans.

The place was hopping, so he'd sent Valentina over to secure them a table and of course Zeke had wanted to go with her and show her his library books.

Tanner had been ready to tell him no, but Valentina looked pretty pleased about the idea, so he'd let it go. Now they were both bent over one of the books, Valentina's long, dark hair cascading down like a curtain, hiding most of the honey color of Zeke's hair from view.

It was such a cozy sight to see the two of them huddled together in the warm coffee shop, with snow flurries swirling down outside the window and over the little village beyond. Something about it made Tanner feel almost homesick, even though that made no sense at all.

"How can I help you?" Holly Fields asked from behind the counter with a knowing smile.

He ordered three breakfast sandwiches, two coffees, and a hot chocolate, then paid, hoping the whole time that Holly wouldn't ask him anything about Valentina.

"She's super sweet," Holly said softly as she handed over the two coffees. "Comes in here every morning and always has something nice to say."

"We just work together," he said too loudly.

"Oh," Holly said politely. "Well, I'll bet she's nice to work with."

She is nice to work with, he thought to himself.

"I'll be over with your sandwiches and Zeke's hot chocolate in just a minute," Holly told him.

"Thank you," he said.

He slipped a bill into the tip jar when she turned away, and then headed to the table where Valentina and Zeke were still studying their book.

As he got closer, Tanner could see that it was one of the *Busytown* books. Zeke could read short chapter books these days, but he still loved the Richard Scarry stories about the little town full of workers because they were funny, and there was always something new to find in the pictures.

"I read these when I was a kid too," Valentina was telling Zeke as he set the coffees down.

"Did you love them?" Zeke asked.

"I did love them," Valentina said. "But pigs were my favorite animal, so I used to be a little bit sad when the pig caused an accident."

"Real pigs are very dangerous," Zeke told her solemnly.

"I guess I should keep that in mind since I'm living in the country now," Valentina said. "Thank you, Zeke."

"Holly said this is how you like your coffee," Tanner said, feeling almost like a third wheel as he sat down opposite the two of them. "I grabbed us all breakfast sandwiches too. I hope you don't mind."

"Are you kidding?" Valentina said. "That sounds great."

She seemed so much more relaxed today. She still wore high heeled boots and a sweater that looked like it might have cost more than Tanner's first car, but she had jeans on and her long hair was down.

Honestly though, Tanner suspected it was the company that had her guard down. Zeke had that effect on people. And he clearly really liked Valentina. The two of them leaned toward each other slightly, though he wasn't even sure they were aware of it.

"Okay, I've got a not-too-hot hot chocolate here," Holly announced as she arrived at their table with a full tray. "And three breakfast sandwiches."

"*Yes*," Zeke said, causing Holly to laugh as she placed his mug in front of him and handed out the sandwiches.

The food smelled incredible and tasted even better, and for a few minutes there was absolute silence at the table as they all enjoyed their meal.

"Okay," Tanner said when his sandwich was gone. "Valentina and I are going to talk about something important for a little while, buddy. Will you be okay reading while we do that?"

"Sure, Dad," Zeke said, then took another giant bite of his sandwich.

"Good job," Tanner said, his heart so full it felt like it was going to explode as he looked at his boy.

This was one of the things they didn't warn you about parenthood, how occasionally your child would fill your heart so suddenly that you couldn't catch your breath—for almost no reason at all.

"What did you mean before?" Valentina asked. "When you said that everything I needed to know was right there in the papers?"

He turned his attention to the woman he couldn't seem to get out of his thoughts lately. She might look relaxed today, but it was clear that she was as focused as ever. She definitely wasn't losing sleep thinking about him.

But he couldn't bring himself to blame her for that. She was loyal to her boss to a fault. And he wasn't going to knock anyone for loyalty.

"Look," he said, "I know the paper seems to only report good news. And that's kind of the town personality too."

"Like, *look on the bright side*?" she asked.

"Exactly," he said, nodding. "We try and look on the bright side as much as we can. After all, life is pretty great here, and there's no reason to complain over things we can't change anyway."

She nodded, looking thoughtful.

"But there's another way to read each article," he went on. "You mentioned a craft fair being rained out. Wouldn't it be nice if there were a covered space for that kind of thing?"

"Oh," she said, grabbing her phone to note down the

idea. "Yes, a space like that would be a great rain-date option for movie nights and pet adoption dates too."

"Absolutely," he said.

"So, a covered space for anything that might get rained out," she said. "I wonder if he could donate land for that to the town. But of course, that doesn't solve the problem of how to get the rest of it sold."

"The newspaper doesn't really tell you everything," Tanner said. "It's probably better to get out there and talk to people."

"Sure," she said. "I could ask people what they'd like to see in town. Although if you aren't thinking about real estate development, you might not even know what you want or need."

"I think you could figure it out by talking with them," Tanner said. "You wouldn't even need to ask specifically about what they needed. You could just get them talking about what challenges they're facing."

Valentina was frowning with concentration as she typed everything he was saying into her phone.

"Here's the thing though," Tanner said, rubbing the back of his neck as he tried to figure out how to tell her without hurting her feelings. "You can't just... march around on high heels, shaking people's hands and asking about their challenges."

She looked up, her eyes wide.

"The best way to get people to open up is to try and match your pace to the town," he went on. "Slow things down, relax and enjoy yourself a little."

She nodded, but even her nod was still brisk and focused.

An idea struck him, maybe the perfect example of what he meant.

"Have you ever been to Cassidy Farm?" he asked, figuring that of course she'd say yes.

"I've heard people talk about it," she said, shaking her head.

"You haven't been to Cassidy Farm," he said, blinking at her stupidly. "But you've been living here for a year."

"I've been busy," she said dismissively, breaking eye contact to look at her phone screen again.

Shoot. He had actually hurt her feelings.

"I'm so glad," he said quickly. "Zeke and I would love to be the first ones to introduce you to the farm. What do you say? Do you have time to go with us tomorrow?"

"Please, Valentina," Zeke said excitedly, his attention definitely distracted from his book now. "It's so awesome there, and I can show you the real corn maze."

"Sure," she said, giving Zeke a warm smile, and then turning to Tanner. "If you guys don't mind?"

"There's no better place at Christmastime," Tanner told her, trying not to lose himself in the welcome sight of her dimples.

10

VALENTINA

Valentina stood in front of the mirror, wondering why it had been so long since she left home looking like she was ready to have fun.

She wore a pretty tan sweater with barely visible white snowflakes woven around the collar and a pair of dark, trouser-style jeans and brown leather, low-heeled granny boots. The whole thing was going to look great with her wool coat.

It had been hard not to notice Tanner's reaction to her hair yesterday. She was wearing it down again today.

It's not to get his attention, she told herself firmly. *It's so that I look relaxed and casual, like he asked.*

She swiped a little gloss on her lips and nodded with satisfaction. She looked pretty and relaxed, but still like herself. If she bumped into anyone she worked with, it wasn't like they would see her looking like a punk rocker or something. She was just dropping the formality for once.

Why don't you call him Baz?

Emma's question lingered in her mind. It had been hard to articulate her answer at the bridesmaids' night. But the more she thought about it, the more Valentina felt that she really wanted respect and formality to be part of her workplace. And Radcliffe must want the same, if she had risen so quickly to the top of his team and he had installed her as his right hand.

And besides, it wasn't as if she didn't have feelings of warmth and admiration for her boss. She absolutely did. Mr. Radcliffe was kind and fair and she honestly adored him. They had known each other for most of her adult life, and she knew him and his son better than she knew most of her extended family members.

But that didn't mean they had to be on a first-name basis. Maybe their closeness made it that much more important that he knew she hadn't forgotten the chain of command. Her dad liked to remind her that the old saying that "familiarity breeds contempt" had been found in writings as far back as the fifth century. Which certainly backed up her desire to stay professional when it came to her boss.

A bright tone chirped from her laptop, and she gasped and ran for the living room.

Valentina had regular video calls with her family every Sunday after early morning church, and she was normally waiting around and looking forward to the sound of that tone. But with all the excitement over her research and the plans she had made with Tanner and Zeke, she had actually forgotten all about today's call.

At least I look nice, she told herself as she lifted the screen of her laptop and accepted the call.

"VAH-lay," the younger of her two older brothers yelled, pronouncing her nickname the Spanish way, and making her smile.

"Hey, Rafe," she said fondly.

"Rafael, is she on?" their mother called from the other room.

"She's here, Mamá," he called back to her.

Just then, another rectangle appeared in the call and her oldest brother Gabriel's face popped up.

"Hey kids," Gabriel said, arching a brow. "Are you behaving?"

"You know you're only like two years older than me," Rafe reminded him.

"And I always will be," Gabriel replied with a satisfied smile.

Valentina laughed. She loved the constant joking around between Rafe and Gabriel that had been the soundtrack to her childhood.

Their mom squeezed in beside Rafe, the two of them taking up one of the three rectangles. Normally, her parents shared a laptop and Rafe used his own from somewhere else in the house.

"Where's Papá?" Valentina asked.

"The VanHorns up on the ninth floor have a leak in their ceiling again," Mama said brightly, shaking her head and looking like she was trying not to laugh.

"The Albrechts," Valentina and Gabriel said together.

The Albrechts loved their indoor garden, but Birdy Albrecht was getting older, and she tended to miss the flowerpots when she did her watering these days, which caused problems when she used the hose from out on the balcony, which was strictly prohibited by the lease but didn't seem to stop her.

Valentina's dad, Hugo Jimenez, had earned a business degree in the evenings after working during the day for a general contractor. But before he ever had a single interview for an office position, he had taken a job as superintendent of a fancy uptown apartment building, The Manchester. The job came with a first-floor apartment for his own family that would allow the three Jimenez children to attend one of the very best public schools in the city.

Now they were all through school, but housing costs had gone up so much that her parents had decided they were better off staying put. But that also meant her father kept losing countless evenings and weekends to the various VanHorns and Albrechts of the building. Valentina couldn't count how many Christmas Eves and Easter dinners had been interrupted when someone at The Manchester called on her father for *just a silly thing* that took him hours to sort out, and could have easily waited for Monday.

Valentina was certain that after all of her father's sacrifice, her parents expected all three kids to make something of themselves.

Gabriel had become a teacher, and while there was no more noble profession, it didn't pay well. So, while they were incredibly proud of their oldest, Valentina was pretty sure he wasn't going to be able to help out their parents financially, especially once he had a family of his own.

Rafael had been accepted to law school. But he'd fallen in love with art during a semester abroad in his senior year of undergrad, and he'd wound up going to Paris to study art instead. Now he was living at home again and gearing up for another of his shows. Again, their parents were proud of Rafe's skills and passion. But Valentina still worried.

By the time she headed to college, she knew it was all down to her. Her parents would never say it, but if anyone was going to get them into their own apartment, and her father off his knees on other people's floors, it was her.

And she was *so close.*

"How are you, Valentina?" her mom asked.

The others looked at her expectantly.

"Things here are good," she said. "Overall, at least. Mr. Radcliffe really needs to sell some properties to get this project into the black. I'm researching ways he could do that without feeling like he let the town down."

"I meant how are *you*, honey," her mom said, a furrow in her brow.

"Oh, I'm fine," Valentina said, racking her brain for something personal to tell them and realizing happily that she *did* have something this week. "I was at a get-together for the bridesmaids a few nights ago. We tried on dresses and ate dinner together."

"That sounds like fun," her mother said.

"It was," Valentina told her. "We were at Natalie's house. Her mother-in-law made all the dresses, and she cooked our dinner too. She made it all look so easy."

"That's really nice," her mom said. "Reminds me of your abuela."

"Oh, you're right," Valentina said, nodding and realizing that was why she had felt so at home that night.

"Is Emma getting nervous about the wedding?" her mom asked. "It's coming up soon."

"No," Valentina said, smiling fondly. "She just seems happy."

"She's marrying Mr. Moneybags," Rafe teased, his eyes dancing. "She's only nervous he'll change his mind."

"That's *not* why she's marrying him," Valentina protested.

He was teasing, but she knew they all wondered. She wished they could meet her friend so they would understand. Valentina knew how it looked for a young woman from a struggling family to marry a man as wealthy as Mr. Radcliffe. But it hadn't taken Valentina long to see that Emma was the most sincere and least greedy person she had ever met.

"Rafael, you apologize to your sister," Mom said sternly. "That's her friend."

"Sorry," Rafe said contritely. "But I still think you should have made him fall in love with you instead."

"That's not how love works, papi," Mom said, shaking her head with a smile.

"Why don't you make one of your rich art patronesses fall in love with you, Rafe?" Gabriel teased. "If money is so important."

"As soon as I get some rich art patronesses, I'll definitely marry one of them," Rafe said dreamily. "As long as she can cook."

"*Rafael,*" their mother said, smacking his shoulder. But she was smiling. They all knew Rafael was a true romantic. He would never marry for money, or even for good home-cooked meals.

Valentina's doorbell rang before she had time to say anything else.

Tanner...

"I want to stay and hear about what's going on with everyone," Valentina said. "But I actually have to run."

"Do you have a date?" Gabriel asked suddenly.

Gabriel was the last member of the family who would ever tease her for not having a social life. And he was also the most perceptive.

Oh, Gabriel—you and your oldest brother superpower...

She blinked at the screen, feeling her face heat, and then started shaking her head hard.

"No," she said. "Definitely not. I'm taking a little research trip with a coworker."

Actually, he's an independent contractor. And he reports to me. And I wish it was a date, even though I ran HR's Appropriate-Workplace sessions myself back in the city...

"Ohhhhh," Rafe crowed. "A *coworker*, huh? I thought All-Business-Valentina would never date a co-worker."

"I wouldn't," she said quickly. "I've got to go, though. I love you guys."

She logged out as they were all yelling their goodbyes.

Sometimes she missed her family so much it hurt. She wished they could all be in the same city. But she was super thankful that they had their regular video calls. Seeing them all happy like that made it worth being teased mercilessly by her brothers every Sunday.

She grabbed her coat and her bag and headed down the steps to the main entry.

Tanner stood outside looking absolutely gorgeous with his cowboy hat and faded jeans. Zeke was bundled up, but she could see his smiling face peeking out from between his hat and scarf.

"Hey there," Tanner said, his deep voice sending a little shiver through her.

"Hi, Valentina," Zeke said. "We're going to have so much fun today, and we're definitely getting a candy apple."

"We *might* get a candy apple," Tanner corrected him. "If we do a good job having a real lunch first."

"Okay," Zeke agreed. "I lost a tooth, Valentina."

He grinned at her, and she saw that sure enough, one of the teeth beside the two front ones that were growing in was now missing.

"Wow," she said.

"The tooth fairy left me a dollar," he said. "So I can buy my own candy apple."

"The tooth fairy doesn't know about inflation," Tanner teased. "Or she would have a good plan there for getting more teeth."

"What's inflation?" Zeke asked.

"I'll explain it to you later," Tanner told him. "Right now, I'm worried about Valentina's coat."

"My coat?" Valentina asked, looking down at herself.

"That's a very pretty coat," Tanner said. "But we're going to the farm. Do you have one that's more casual? One you can throw in the washing machine if it gets dirty?"

"No," she said. "I guess I'll just have to take my chances."

"Nah," Tanner said. "Here."

He shrugged off the thick fleece jacket he wore and handed it to her.

"Oh, I couldn't—" she began.

"I've got another one in the truck," he told her, grabbing a fleece-lined flannel from the backseat. "You can put your pretty one back here."

"Okay," she told him, taking off her coat and handing it over.

It was bitterly cold out, but Tanner's emerald green, fleece jacket was still warm with his body heat. And it smelled like wood fires and spice, just like his sweater had.

He likes me wearing his clothes, a little voice whispered in the back of her head.

But that couldn't really be it. He just wanted her to look casual, like everyone else. And he didn't want her to have a big dry-cleaning bill if she got messy. It was very thoughtful of him, and generous to share his jacket. He was a good man. That was all.

"Are you so excited to see a corn maze, Valentina?" Zeke asked as he climbed into his booster seat in the back.

"I can't wait," she told him.

Tanner had walked around to the passenger door and was holding it open for her, looking like a cowboy hero in a movie.

She felt her cheeks heat as she climbed in, making sure to look anywhere but into his eyes.

Pull it together, she told herself. *The man is just trying to help. You have to stop noticing how handsome he is.*

11

VALENTINA

After a peaceful drive, Valentina stood in the parking lot of Cassidy Farm, looking around as Tanner helped Zeke out of the backseat.

Huge sycamore trees lined the parking lot, their peeling bark in tones of brown and white making them beautiful, though their branches were bare.

Tanner had parked up at the top of the lot near a hand-painted sign for hayrides. From their spot, she could look down over a yard full of cut Christmas trees in front of a display area with giant decorations featuring a multitude of homemade characters dressed for the holidays.

A big red octagonal barn at the bottom of the hill had open shelves by the entry, with hundreds of beautiful scarlet poinsettias displayed on them.

"The Christmas All-Year-Round shop is upstairs in the barn," Tanner said as he and Zeke joined her. "You'll love it."

"Melody works there," she said, wondering if she might bump into her fellow bridesmaid today.

"It smells good in there," Zeke pointed out.

"I can't wait," she told the beaming boy. His smile was even cuter than usual with his missing tooth.

"Ready to look around?" Tanner asked.

"Absolutely," she said.

For a second it almost felt like he was going to take her hand, and there was an awkward beat as she adjusted. But as soon as they headed down the gravel lot to all the farm's attractions, she felt relaxed again.

It was cold enough out to see their breath, but there was no sign of snow flurries today. As long as they kept moving, she was pretty sure she wouldn't freeze. And it sounded like they would be going inside some too, which was good.

"Let's go to the corn maze," Zeke said excitedly.

"Okay, bud," Tanner told him. "But that's all the way on the far side of the farm. Are you sure you won't need to stop any place in between?"

"I'm sure," Zeke told him.

Tanner looked over at Valentina and winked. She figured there must be a lot of things Zeke liked between here and there.

Trinity Falls was such a small community, and the farmhouses were so spread out. Valentina wouldn't have thought it could support a big place like this.

But the parking lot was more than half full, and families pulled strollers and wheelchairs out of the backs of their station wagons and headed cheerfully toward the trees, the barn, and whatever was beyond.

"Hi, Miss Jimenez," a familiar voice said.

"Hey, Jessie," she said, smiling at the young guy from one of the paint crews.

He was here with a little girl—maybe his baby sister? They each carried a gallon of what had to be apple cider. Jessie's hung effortlessly from his hand, but the girl was struggling proudly with hers.

"We're going to see Grandma," the little girl said, panting a bit.

"Can't show up empty-handed," Jessie said with a crooked smile.

"Well, you definitely aren't doing that," Valentina told them. "I'll bet she'll be super excited to see all that fresh apple cider."

"See you both," Jessie said as they headed up into the parking area.

"Who was that?" Zeke asked.

"Jessie is someone I work with," Valentina said, feeling happy about having been recognized. "I would have introduced you guys, but they were carrying all that heavy cider."

"I know Jessie," Tanner said. "He's a little younger than me, but I know a couple of his cousins."

"Oh," Valentina said, rethinking Jessie's crooked smile.

Would rumors start swirling Monday that she was spending time outside of work with Tanner? In retrospect, maybe this didn't look good...

"He won't say anything about seeing us together," Tanner said after a moment. "If that's bothering you."

"We're researching ways to use Mr. Radcliffe's land," Valentina said. "There's nothing to be ashamed of."

"True," Tanner said thoughtfully. "I guess we've got nothing to worry about."

She could feel the friendly atmosphere between the three of them start to cool a tiny bit.

"*And* we're here to have fun together," she added. "Right, Zeke?"

"Do you have any kids?" Zeke asked her suddenly.

She glanced over at Tanner, who had a funny look on his face, though she wasn't sure why. Little kids didn't know how this stuff worked. Zeke's own dad was clearly a single parent.

"I don't," she said. "I live by myself, so today is super special for me."

"All by yourself?" Zeke asked sadly.

"Well," she said, horrified that it sounded pathetic enough for a seven-year-old to feel sorry for her, "I like to read and crochet, so it's sort of nice to have my own little apartment where I can do quiet things."

"Like the reading nook in kindergarten," Zeke said, nodding wisely. "I bet you have a lot of pillows at your apartment."

"I *do* have a lot of pillows," Valentina said, laughing. "How about you?"

"I live with just my dad," Zeke said. "My mom doesn't feel like being a parent anymore."

"Whoa," Tanner said, looking alarmed. "That's not— where did you hear that?"

"Uncle Axel said it to Grandma," Zeke said, looking a

little sad. *"It's bad enough she doesn't want to be a parent anymore, but can't she at least send him some toys?"*

Valentina swallowed over a lump in her throat. That sounded like the kind of thing Zeke would have overheard on his birthday or on Christmas—a time when he was getting presents. It must have hurt his heart to hear those things being said about his mom not wanting to be there for him.

"You know Uncle Axel just likes to talk a lot of trash, right, bud?" Tanner asked Zeke, crouching to look him in the eye.

"Yeah," Zeke said, nodding, but still looking sad.

"Like all that stuff he says when the Eagles play Dallas?" Tanner added. "Stuff we know he doesn't really mean?"

Zeke nodded again, but he still looked down at his feet.

"And if you had any more toys, could they even fit in your room?" Tanner asked.

Zeke looked thoughtful for a moment and then he grinned at his dad and shook his head.

"See?" Tanner said. "Uncle Axel was just making a lot of noise. When your mom can get away, I know she'll come visit you. She's staying busy, and that's a good thing. It means she's happy, right?"

Zeke nodded up and down.

"Besides," Tanner told him with a flash of mischief in his eyes, "I'm not sure I want to share you anyway. I want all your little bear hugs for myself."

He grabbed his son and swept him up in his arms, spinning him around while he growled like a big bear, totally unconcerned about the people around them who were staring as they headed to and from their cars.

Zeke shrieked with laughter and growled back, clearly delighted.

Valentina felt tears brimming in her eyes, and did her best to blink them back. Seeing the two of them like this was making her heart ache, and she wasn't really sure why.

"Okay, look out corn maze," Tanner said, setting his son back on the ground. "Here we come."

But as they walked, there were so many things that caught Zeke's attention, just as Tanner had predicted.

Good smells emanated from the big barn that Tanner explained had been turned into a store and bakery. Zeke decided he could wait and get cider to bring home at the end of the day.

They passed through an open area with picnic tables surrounded by booths selling candied apples, funnel cakes, and more. There was even a man selling soft pretzels from a cart. Zeke smacked his lips, but remained determined to go to the corn maze first.

When they got to a paddock where a young man was leading around a big pony with a small girl on its back Zeke got excited enough that he was practically quivering.

"We can do a quick pony ride first if you want," Tanner offered.

Valentina bit her lip, wondering if she might be allowed to take one too, and get a few pointers from the guy leading them around. But obviously that wouldn't be allowed.

And besides, even though Tanner and the sign both called it a pony, it still seemed like such a big animal.

I'm sorry, Abuelo, she told her grandfather in her mind. *I'm so close to your dream, but I'm such a coward.*

She might be able to chicken out today, but she was going to have to face her fears really soon when it came time for Emma's wedding.

"You okay?" Tanner asked. "Did you... want to feed the pony?"

"Oh," she said, feeling silly for staring at the paddock for too long. "No, no, I was just thinking of my grandfather."

"Was he a rider?" Tanner asked.

"No," she admitted. "But he always wanted to be one."

"So I guess your parents taught you, then?" Tanner asked.

She blinked at him for a second.

"Sorry," he said. "It's just that I saw the little statue on your desk, so I know you're a horse person."

"Oh," she said, laughing nervously. "Yes, I do like to keep him on my desk. He belonged to my grandfather."

"The ducks," Zeke yelled, saving her for the moment. "Can we feed the ducks right away after we do the corn maze?"

"Sure," Tanner said. "If Valentina wants to. She's our guest, remember?"

"Do you want to feed the ducks, Valentina?" Zeke asked hopefully. "It's really fun, and you can get seeds from the little machine and stand on the bridge and throw them down and all the ducks swim around quacking."

"I *definitely* want to do that," she told him sincerely. Feeding the ducks was absolutely her speed.

"*Yes,*" Zeke said, jumping up and down.

"Okay, we're almost there," Tanner told him. "If you want to run ahead, you can. But you have to wait at the gate."

Valentina looked around and saw that although the farm was fairly crowded, this section was almost empty. Tanner would be able to see Zeke all the way to the gate he was talking about.

It hit her suddenly that there were hundreds of tiny assessments and decisions Tanner had probably been making all along—just for a simple day out with his son.

"You want to run too?" Tanner asked her.

She glanced over and saw he was grinning down at her.

"Sorry," she said. "I guess I'm in my own head a lot today."

"You're taking it all in," he said. "There's a lot going on here."

"You're such an amazing dad," she told him suddenly. "He's a really lucky kid."

"Thanks," Tanner said, looking down as they walked. "He deserves it."

"He sure does," she said, watching Zeke finish his sprint and grab onto the gate with both hands, as if willing himself to hold on and not go through it without them.

"His uncle wasn't exactly wrong," Tanner said. "I don't want to lie to Zeke, but I can't stand for him to think anything bad about his mama. The truth is that we got married young, and she just wasn't ready. She's not a bad person. It's not the way my brother makes it sound."

"You were ready though," Valentina heard herself say.

"Yeah," he said, glancing down at her with a smile. "I'm really happy to be a dad. I'll always be grateful to her for giving me Zeke."

She felt her heart opening even more to this man who still valiantly defended his ex-wife, in spite of their unusual situation.

He's loyal, she thought to herself with satisfaction. *I like that.*

"Come on," Zeke yelled to them as they got close, his face radiant with joy. "The corn maze is *right there*, Valentina."

She laughed and jogged over to join him, her heart light at the chance to spend time with the enthusiastic little boy.

A FEW HOURS LATER, Valentina was tired but feeling very happy. It had taken most of her resolve to remember to keep track of all the things the place had to offer instead of just having fun.

They had enjoyed the corn maze. The first time, Zeke held her hand and led her through. After that, they all chased each other.

Feeding the ducks was as much fun as she expected, and they stopped to see the pigs and chickens in their pens too.

The Christmas All-Year-Round store was full of beautiful holiday ornaments, wreaths, and even some local handicrafts, including candles made by one of the second-grade teachers at Zeke's school. And Melody had been there to greet her by name, once again giving Valentina the wonderful feeling of being part of Trinity Falls.

The big store on the main floor below was full of delicious produce grown at Cassidy Farm and some smaller nearby farms. Zeke looked at all the wooden puzzles and toys with Valentina while Tanner slipped off to buy cider and doughnuts that were still warm when they sat at a picnic bench outside to eat them.

"This was amazing," Valentina said. "Thank you both for bringing me. I can't believe I haven't been here before."

"Oh, we love any reason to come here," Tanner said. "Right, Zeke?"

"Yes," Zeke said with his mouth full of doughnut.

They were just cleaning up and getting ready to head out when another man in a cowboy hat jogged over to them.

"Tanner," he called out. "Hang on."

"What's up, Shane?" Tanner asked.

"We've got a broken Rudolph, if you want him," Shane said. "Jacob ran over the cord with the mower in the summertime."

"Oh, I can fix that, no problem," Tanner said. "Did you want him back afterward?"

"No, no," Shane said. "He should be out for everyone to enjoy. Mom says she doesn't need anything more than her manger scene anyway. Come on back on your way out."

"We're heading out now," Tanner said. "Do you mind, Valentina? Shane, this is Valentina. She's Baz Radcliffe's right-hand man. Valentina, Shane Cassidy and his family own this place."

"Hi, Shane," Valentina said smiling and trying desperately not to offer to shake his hand. "I loved my visit here today, and I was at your place the other night with Natalie for the dress fittings. Is Alice your mom?"

"Yes," Shane said, smiling.

"Well, I *really* love your mom," Valentina said. "I'm one of Emma's bridesmaids, so I got to try on the dress she made and eat her corned beef and cabbage, and hear her funny stories."

"Lucky," Tanner said, clucking his tongue.

"Everyone loves her," Shane said, shaking his head as if he were as much in awe of the woman as Valentina was. "Well, she'll be glad to see you again when you come back to the house. Nice to meet you."

Shane gave them a wave and headed back into the big barn.

"You fit right in around here," Tanner said, shaking his own head as they walked back to the car.

"Really?" she asked, feeling surprised.

"You said hello to almost as many people as we did today," he told her. "And Alice Cassidy has made you a piece of clothing. I think that might make you an honorary Trinity Falls-ian."

Valentina laughed as they got in the truck, letting

Tanner open her door and help her up without any awkwardness now that she was ready for it.

A few minutes later, they had followed the driveway past the *Private Property* sign to the old farmhouse on the edge of the Christmas tree farm where the Cassidy family lived. She'd passed by the other night on her way to Shane and Natalie's home just a bit further down.

Alice and her husband, Joe, were standing on the porch as if they had somehow known company was coming.

"Hey there," Joe called to them. "You here for Rudolph?"

"We sure are," Tanner said.

"Oh, my goodness, is that Valentina?" Alice called to them. "And is Zeke with you?"

"Yes," Zeke squeaked from the backseat, but Valentina guessed that Alice probably couldn't hear him.

"Hang, on, buddy," Tanner told him as he parked the truck.

"Do you mind if we go up and say hey for a minute?" he asked Valentina.

"Of course not," she said, feeling happy for the chance to say hello too.

She waited while he opened up the door for Zeke, and the three of them headed up to the porch together.

"There he is," Joe said sadly, pointing at the decoration in the corner. It was probably two feet tall and nicely painted. "Jacob ran over the cord. That boy can be a little reckless."

"No problem," Tanner said, laughing. "We'll just take him back to our workshop, right, Zeke?"

"Yes," Zeke said, smiling proudly.

"Well, he'll have his moment of fame in town then," Joe said fondly.

Valentina wondered suddenly if they meant the lawn next to her building in town. Someone had set up a ton of light-up Christmas characters there recently. Did Tanner have something to do with that?

"Don't you look lovely today?" Alice said to Valentina before she could question Tanner. "What brings you out here?"

She wrapped an arm around Valentina's shoulder and gave her a light squeeze.

"I wanted to learn more about Trinity Falls so I can help Mr. Radcliffe decide what to do with some of the land he's having trouble selling," Valentina told her. "And Tanner was stunned that I hadn't been to Cassidy Farm before. Me too, now that I've seen it. I think I'll be visiting a lot more often now. It's such a special place."

"We love it with all our hearts," Alice told her with a big smile. "I'm so glad you had fun."

"If you're wanting to learn more about Trinity Falls, you have to take a carriage ride at the Hometown Holiday celebration," Joe said. "And you ought to go over to Timber Run and talk to Lucy Webb. She can tell you all about the Co-op Grocer's."

"It's Lucy Beck now, Dad. But Zeke and I would be more than happy to take you over to see her," Tanner offered, a hopeful look in his eyes. "And obviously, we love a good carriage ride. You can't miss the Hometown Holiday celebration."

"Yes, Valentina," Zeke said. "Will you do all that stuff with us?"

"Of course," she heard herself say happily. "I'd love to."

"*Yes,*" Zeke said, flashing his missing-tooth grin again.

His exuberance was catching, and she found herself smiling back so hard it made her cheeks ache. She had a feeling that she might have been smiling at more than just Zeke, but she wasn't going to think about it right now.

12

TANNER

That afternoon, Tanner walked around the lawn beside the apartment building, checking on the decorations and picking up a candy cane wrapper a child must have dropped last night, as well as the handful of dry leaves that invariably blew in here and there.

It was still cold enough that he could see his breath, but the air was fresh and sweet, and besides, he looked forward to this project all year. It made him think of setting up Santa Claus in the yard with his dad when he was a child.

Valentina had asked if he was in charge of these decorations when they were on their way home from Cassidy Farm and he'd been surprised that she didn't know already that he was. It reminded him that she really hadn't been in town all that long.

The lawn ornaments had started out as a labor of love, and then practically become his calling card. Now people started asking him about it the weekend the candy canes went on the lampposts, and donated decorations all year long.

Apparently Valentina had only just started renting her apartment in the building on the other side of the yard. She told him that she had seen the light display on her way home every night, and admired it without ever knowing it was his pet project.

He'd impulsively asked her over tonight to help him set up the new Rudolph, surprising himself by inviting her when he'd turned down all offers of help in the past.

He'd been even more surprised when she said yes right away.

It was only after he'd dropped her off and gotten home himself that he remembered Zeke had a sleepover at the library tonight. He'd earned a spot in the annual overnight lock-in by reading a truly impressive number of books.

The two of them had hustled to pack up Zeke's backpack and sleeping bag, getting to the library just in time for Tanner to get back home and rewire the Rudolph before Valentina was supposed to arrive.

In a way, it was a good thing that he hadn't had time to overthink things. He was already spending too much time daydreaming about her.

It's not a date, he reminded himself for the hundredth time.

But maybe he wished it was a date.

Given that he reported to her, that could be tricky for professional reasons. But it was actually more worrisome for personal ones. He hadn't dated since Karen left. Being there for Zeke and running his business was plenty of work. And besides, he already felt like if he'd failed with his high school sweetheart, so how was he supposed to make it work with someone he only just met?

He'd known Karen inside and out—her family, her history, everything about her. That was why he couldn't really blame her for running off. He'd also known that she was still basically a big kid herself when they got married. She was sweet as pie, but she changed her mind with the weather.

Compared to how fully he'd known Karen, he hardly knew Valentina at all.

I know she's loyal, the little voice whispered to him.

And did he really need to know anything else, when she had such an instant and unusual connection with Zeke, and when he could tell by every single interaction they had that she was thoughtful and kind?

But none of that mattered. What mattered was that he had steady work for once, and that meant he was being a good dad to Zeke.

No getting romantic with her, he chided himself. *Just show her the decorations, like she wanted.*

"Hi," a soft voice said from down on the sidewalk, snapping him out of his thoughts.

"Come on in," he told her, indicating the two steps that led to the decorative, knee-high iron gate.

It was late afternoon, so the decorations weren't lit up yet. But he still saw the smile teasing the corners of her lips as she looked around. No one's inner child would be able to resist a display like this.

She was still in her casual clothing from earlier in the

day. And she was still wearing his jacket, which gave him a funny little flare of pleasure.

"They're not on yet," she said as she stepped into the garden.

"I like to do my check before it gets dark and the lights go on," he told her. "So you're just in time today."

"Where's Zeke?" she asked, looking around like she missed his boy. The thought sent a lick of warmth through his chest.

"We forgot that he had a sleepover at the library tonight," he told her. "I got him over there just before you came."

"Oh, did he win the reading contest?" she asked, sounding impressed.

"He did," Tanner said, smiling. "How did you know?"

"I always did those when I was a kid," Valentina confided, her dimples popping as she smiled at the memory. "I noticed the flyer at the library when I was over there. He's going to have so much fun."

"Miss Caroline really does them up," Tanner said, nodding. "And I know she'll keep him safe and sound."

Valentina looked away, but her smile deepened.

"What?" he asked.

"Oh, it's just I can tell you're worried anyway," she told him. "Even though I'll bet not one bad thing has happened in that library in the whole history of this town."

"The original library burned down, and they had to build a new one," he offered.

"That happened in the 1800s," she said, shaking her

head. "And the building was wood frame back then. Now it's solid brick."

"You've done your homework," he conceded.

"And I'm guessing the wiring in there is better now?" she added.

"It is," he agreed, unable to help smiling back at her. "I had an excuse to check it all out when I installed the electric car charger in the municipal lot."

"You see?" she said. "He's going to be fine. But I don't blame you for worrying. That's kind of your main job, right?"

"Yeah," he said, rubbing the back of his neck. "I try not to let him see it, but the world looks a whole lot more dangerous the minute you have a child."

"I could definitely see that," she agreed. "And he's such a special boy, you've got to keep him safe so he can grow up and make the world a better place."

"You really think he's bright?" Tanner asked, looking up to see the thoughtful smile on her face.

"It's not just that he's bright," she said. "It's that he's excited about new ideas, and he's big-hearted."

"I've got to get him through this year with Mrs. Hastings without him losing his confidence," Tanner confessed. "She gives him so much work, and then she's disappointed if he doesn't get it all done."

"Give her a little time," Valentina predicted. "She'll see him the way we do before the year is over."

Tanner nodded. It felt so good to *talk* about this stuff with someone else who knew Zeke, even a little. He didn't like worrying his parents, who already worried over him being a single dad. And Axel was great, but he had a big mouth and saw things in black and white, rather than the shades of gray Tanner had noticed the world was painted in as he got older.

"So, what do we do?" Valentina asked, looking around like she was ready to roll up her sleeves and dig a trench or rewire a lamp socket if he asked.

"First we just walk the yard and look for trash and dry leaves," he said, trying to hide his smile. "I had just started when you got here."

"Okay," she said. "Where should I start?"

"Why don't you start in the left row?" he offered. "I'll start on the right and we'll work our way back."

"Okay," she told him, her dimples popping.

"If you see a worn or damaged cord let me know," he told her.

"Of course," she said.

They each moved between the figures, and he noticed how she stopped at each one to study the cord.

"So, you manage the building?" she asked after a few minutes, her eyes on a big plastic elf.

"Yep," he told her. "I wanted to have a home in town for Zeke, and managing the place means we only pay half the regular rent."

She nodded, and he couldn't help noticing the furrow in her brow.

Maybe she didn't like the idea that he was budget conscious. But not everyone had a fancy business school degree and money to spend on designer clothing.

"My dad is the super in the building where I grew up," she said suddenly. "For the same reason as you, actually. He wanted my brothers and me to go to the best public school."

"Wow," Tanner said, truly surprised.

"Yeah," she said, looking almost worried, like he was going to judge her or something.

"I guess your dad and I have a lot in common then," he managed, giving her a smile. "It says a lot about a person when they do what they need to do for their kids to grow up happy."

"It's hard though, right?" she said. "I mean do the tenants always interrupt your evenings and weekends?"

"There are only eight apartments," he said, frowning. "But, yes, I mean, I've been called in nights and weekends, and sometimes even for easy stuff like changing a light bulb."

"Tell me about it," Valentina said, frowning.

"Well, Mrs. Ying is by herself now," he said. "And she's very small and frail. It isn't a good idea for her to change lightbulbs anymore. And she always feeds Zeke dumplings when we go up there. She's a good neighbor."

Valentina smiled up at him, looking a little surprised.

"What?" he asked.

"You just reminded me of the Albrechts in our building," she said, shrugging. "Birdy had this big tin of hard candy when I was little. It was made in the prettiest ripples. She always sent me home with some wrapped in a napkin when I went up to her place with my dad."

"See?" Tanner said. "It feels really good to be appreciated."

"Oh, look at that," she said suddenly.

He moved to her and saw that the cords for an angel

and a Mrs. Claus, that were on opposite sides of the aisle had been set loose from the loops he secured the excess cord length in, and were tangled together.

"Ah," he said. "This is exactly the kind of thing we're looking for. Good eye."

"What happened to them?" she asked, crouching beside him.

"Teenagers, probably," he said, shrugging. "Maybe they thought they could steal one and then changed their mind when their conscience struck, or if someone walked by. Or maybe they were just fooling around. At any rate, I have to take care of it because someone could trip."

"Okay," Valentina said.

He went over to the nearest raised exterior outlet and found the tagged cords that went with each decoration and unplugged them.

By the time he got back, Valentina had made considerable progress untangling the wires. He watched her finish up and then looped the cords and re-secured them himself before plugging them back in.

"Nice work," he told her.

"Thanks," she said, grinning up at him.

"So, you have brothers?" he couldn't resist asking.

He was trying to put her together in his mind again. With the way she dressed and spoke and carried herself, he would never have guessed she had grown up sort of like Zeke.

"They're both older than me," she said, nodding. "Rafe—Rafael is an artist. And Gabriel is a teacher."

"Your parents must be really proud of you three," Tanner said.

She gave him an odd look and then nodded.

"What was that?" he asked.

"Well, I mean, none of us are exactly making their sacrifices pay off," she said, shrugging.

"I disagree," Tanner said. "The world needs art and children need teachers. And you're helping Baz do some amazing things out here."

She nodded, but she still had that furrow in her brow.

He was trying to think of a way to draw her out and maybe help her look at things differently, when she moved closer to his row.

"What's that—" she began, and promptly tripped over something.

Her hair lifted as she flew through the air, and Tanner moved as quickly as he could, automatically catching her in his arms before she could tumble into a gathering of plastic snowmen.

Suddenly, the delicate scent of lilac filled his senses and the world around them disappeared as he enveloped her small, soft form in his arms.

Her beautiful eyes were fixed on his when he gazed down, her pink lips slightly parted in surprise. Time seemed to stand still and everything in him felt *pulled* to her, as if there were a kind of gravity between them, dragging them toward each other instead of to the ground. He felt like if his lips touched hers they might actually float above the garden.

"Tanner," she murmured, her expression softer than he had ever seen it.

A loud click sounded and every single figure in the

display lit up all at once, filling the yard around them with brilliant light.

"Oh," she said, letting out a surprised little laugh that would be burned into his heart forever. "Oh, wow."

Time began to move again, and he realized he was holding her in his arms in the middle of the light display.

She seemed to realize it at the same time. She pulled back slightly and then looked down at her boot.

"I'm really tangled up," she said, shaking her head. "Sorry I came flying at you like that."

"No problem," he said, feeling like he should be glad the lights had come on and saved him from a big mistake, but secretly wishing he'd scheduled them to come on just a few minutes later. "Let me get you out of there."

Kneeling at her feet while she laughed at herself, he couldn't help the image that flashed in his mind of him kneeling to slide a ring onto her finger.

Stop that, he told himself. *She's just a nice girl who wants to make her parents proud. She didn't come here for you to moon over her.*

But he had a feeling he wouldn't be able to help replaying tonight in his mind over and over again, wondering what might have happened and what it would have meant.

13

VALENTINA

Valentina moved around her apartment, cleaning and dusting—just as she did each day after work.

Her apartment never really got a chance to get very messy, but the ritual calmed her spirit and helped her make the transition from work time to relaxing at home, even if she normally brought at least a little work home.

Besides, she loved the fresh pine scent from the wood cleaner she used on the floors. Today it was blending with the spice of the cinnamon candle she had burning on the kitchen counter—making the whole place smell like Christmas.

She thought again about getting a tree for her little space.

She peeked out her front window at the snowflakes drifting down, and saw there were fewer trees for sale on the lawn outside the library. But the big town tree was right there. When it was lit up, she would be able to see it from the window.

And she could see Tanner and Zeke's lights from the bathroom window.

She had spent the last few days alternately telling herself not to think about Tanner Williams, and indulging in wild fantasies where he actually kissed her in the middle of the Christmas light display.

He wasn't going to kiss me, she tried telling herself again.

But she was pretty sure he'd been thinking about it. The way he had held her, so gently, like she was something precious, his eyes on hers like he was trying to read what was written on her soul, before they slid down to her mouth.

And then the whole garden had lit up all at once.

Just thinking about it made her smile. It was like magic—like the universe had stepped in to shine a spotlight on the fact that they were perfect together.

No, she reminded herself sternly. *We both work for Mr. Radcliffe and it's not right to think of Tanner that way.*

But she was having a hard time not thinking of him almost constantly. And it wasn't like she could avoid him when they were about to head over to the Webb family's farm together to meet everyone and to talk with Lucy Beck about the Co-op Grocer's.

Valentina knew she should be looking forward to having a frank conversation with Lucy about whether there was anything lacking at the Co-op.

But honestly, she was just excited to see Tanner and Zeke again. This wouldn't be like going to Cassidy Farm and watching the seven-year-old dash from activity to activity, showing her everything he could do, and everything he thought she would like. It would be nice to have a quiet evening with a big family.

She missed her big brothers more and more lately. Maybe that was Tanner and Zeke's effect on her. All that jubilant male energy reminded her of her brothers' childhood antics. They had roped Valentina into their silly pranks more often than not, and her mom always scolded them for being a bad influence on their little sister. But looking back, Valentina also remembered her mom trying not to smile as she did.

Mom liked having her included back then, and she was finding that she liked to be included now too.

She wiped down the kitchen counters and blew out the candle before heading to her room to grab some clothes to put on after she showered.

Sadly, she didn't have a lot of casual options. Most of her wardrobe was either work clothing or cozy pajamas. While she searched clearance racks and doubled up on coupons for work clothes that looked professional but didn't cost an arm and a leg, Valentina treated herself when it came to warm pajamas for hanging out at home —after all, they weren't nearly as expensive. Her current favorite was a fleece set in a red and white Nordic print that made her think of candy canes.

She grabbed a pair of dark jeans and a camel-colored sweater and laid them on the bed before heading into the bathroom for a quick shower.

Once the water was steamy warm, she got in. From inside her bathtub, if she went up on her toes, she could just see out the small, high window that overlooked the lawn between the two apartment buildings.

The decorations there weren't lit up yet, but they would be soon. The garden still looked so cheerful, especially with the early snow blanketing the whole lawn. She wondered how much happier the residents in both buildings felt each time they walked past and saw the display. Some tenants even had windows that faced the garden. She imagined it would be lovely to look out at the brilliant holiday sight.

She showered quickly and was dressed and ready by the time her doorbell rang, making her heart skip a beat.

It's not like that, she tried to remind her heart.

She grabbed her bag and headed downstairs to find Tanner outside waiting with Zeke by his side.

"Hi, Valentina," Zeke said before wrapping his arms around her waist. "I'm glad to see you."

"I'm glad to see you too, Zeke," she said, hugging him back.

When he let go, she felt tears prickle her eyes, though she had no idea why. It was just awfully nice to be hugged by Zeke Williams.

"Ready to see Timber Run?" Tanner asked, his deep voice as calm and gentle as always.

"Yes," she said as they headed to his truck. "I hear it's one of the most interesting houses in Trinity Falls."

"Where did you hear that?" Tanner asked.

"Caroline over at the library," she told him.

"Well, Caroline's right," he said, opening the passenger door for her and offering her a hand to get in.

She didn't really need it, but she loved the way it felt when his hand enveloped hers, warm and comforting.

The three of them talked about their day all the way

to the Webbs' farm. Mostly, Zeke told them about the Winter Party plans Mrs. Hastings had for the class. From what Valentina could tell, they weren't exactly having a party for Christmas or Hanukkah, but based on the treats Zeke told them the different kids were bringing in, at least those two holidays would be represented by delicious offerings from home, maybe even more.

"Are you going to a Winter Party, Valentina?" Zeke asked suddenly.

"Well, not really," she told him. "But I always have a video call with my family on holidays."

"I can bring two grownups to my holiday party," Zeke said, a hopeful note in his voice.

"I'll bet they're supposed to be from your family," Valentina said.

"I'm sure Valentina can't take time off work," Tanner said at the same time.

Valentina laughed nervously, uncertain whether she was relieved that Tanner didn't want her there, or hurt, or both.

"Oh," Zeke said sadly. "I'm sorry, Valentina."

"That's okay," she told him. "You can tell me all about it afterward, next time we see each other."

"Here we are," Tanner said, pulling his truck down a long drive.

"Oh," Valentina said, catching sight of what could only be Timber Run. "Oh, wow."

She had privately thought it was a little silly for a house on a farm out in the country to have a name. But seeing the elegant wood and glass of Timber Run rising out of the hillside, she could see instantly that she had been wrong.

"Now, Mrs. Webb is a little particular about her wood floors," Tanner said. "So we'll all give our shoes a good wipe on the porch and then take them off as soon as we go in, okay?"

"Yes," Zeke said seriously.

By the time they all got up to the porch to wipe their shoes, Valentina was more eager than ever to see the inside of the house. Even through two inches of snow, she could see that the porch decking was set at a diagonal angle, and beautiful poinsettias were displayed on a small table. The whole place felt so deliberately simple and beautiful.

"Welcome, welcome," Leticia Webb called to them as she opened the front door. "Come on in."

Rich, savory scents drifted out of the house, as well as the faraway sound of Christmas music.

"We're still in the kitchen," Leticia said. "But make yourselves at home."

"Thank you for having us," Valentina told her as they all came in and slipped off their shoes on the pretty rug next to the door. "I've always wanted to see Timber Run. Everyone says you had a big hand in its design."

"I'm no architect," Leticia replied, her face lit with delight at a chance to talk about her home. "But Simon and I worked with an architect from the city, and he allowed me to put my touches on it. Then the Esh family built the structure."

She knew that name. Mr. Esh and his family were

Amish, but Valentina was learning that they did a lot of building in Trinity Falls.

Since Mr. Radcliffe was mostly just replacing roofing, HVAC, and electrical, they hadn't needed anyone for a big building project yet. But one look at the gorgeous woodwork at Timber Run made her determined to reach out to them if the opportunity ever came up.

"It's exquisite," Valentina told her. "The ceilings are so high."

"They're no fun to dust, let me tell you," Leticia said, shaking her head in mock dismay. But she was clearly tickled.

Ashton Beck, Lucy's husband came up, shook Tanner's hand, and the two of them headed to the kitchen. A little boy who Valentina thought might be Kellan's son, ran up and grabbed Zeke's hand, leading him to the kitchen too.

"I'll just show you to the dining room and Lucy will be right out with some tea and appetizers so you two can chat," Leticia said, leading the way.

"Oh, wow," Valentina sighed.

The whole back wall of the house was floor to ceiling glass, revealing the woods beyond. In the summertime it was probably just a soft haze of green, but right now the bare, silvery branches wore only a mantle of white, allowing a beautiful view of the creek and the snowy bank.

"This is what Simon promised me when he proposed," Leticia said fondly. "If I would come and live on the farm with him, he would give me a modern home with a view of those woods in the back."

"I'm so glad you said yes," Valentina murmured, drinking in the view.

"Me too," Leticia said with a smile. "Don't tell him I said so, but I would have married him even without the pretty house."

"Valentina," Lucy called to her as she came out of the kitchen carrying a tray.

"Let me help you with that, sweetheart," Leticia said, hurrying over to her.

Valentina watched them unload a teapot and two pretty earthenware cups as well as a wooden cutting board with cheese and rectangles of rustic bread.

"Oh, wow," Valentina said. "This looks amazing."

"Well, you won't remember what you talked about if you don't have a little snack," Leticia said, patting Lucy's head absentmindedly as she headed back to the kitchen. "Enjoy, girls."

"Thank you so much for doing this, Lucy," Valentina told her. "I shop at the Co-op, but I've never known much about it. How does it work? Is there anything that would make it better?"

She took a breath and tried to remember to pace herself.

"Well, I guess it's easiest to start with the history," Lucy said with a smile. "Now all this is before I was born, obviously. But when Tom Dudek, my manager, was a kid, he remembers when his dad and a couple of other people in town started the place."

"Oh, wow," Valentina said.

"They would take turns accepting deliveries of fruit, vegetables, grains, dairy, meat, poultry, and so forth from the local farmers early in the mornings," Lucy said. "And they also took turns driving Bennett Harbrook's van into the city for the things we couldn't get around here. The Co-op didn't have everything back then, like it does now. But it had a lot."

"It sounds like a real adventure," Valentina said, privately wondering how they had possibly worked out costs and reimbursements.

"It was a labor of love back then," Lucy said. "As Tom says, it was actually cooperative. Now most folks just pay the one-time investment if they want to help out, and they get their discount on Tuesdays and certain specials in exchange. And workers like me are paid to do the rest. And anyone can come and shop, not just the members."

"I've seen calls for volunteers though," Valentina said.

"Oh, yes," Lucy said with a smile. "People do come and help out from time to time with all kinds of things. The community has been really good to us."

"The reason I wanted to chat with you is that Mr. Radcliffe has some land up near where the highway will be coming in," Valentina said. "You know he's putting a deed restriction on each sale that makes it impossible to convert the properties for commercial use."

Lucy nodded. Everyone knew that by now.

"Well, he's having a hard time finding buyers for it since he's selling built homes that are in nicer locations," Valentina said, pausing for a moment.

"I see," Lucy said, in a way that made Valentina know that she didn't see.

"I'm not here *for* Mr. Radcliffe today," Valentina said carefully. "I just wanted to do a little legwork on my own.

I know everyone loves the Co-op. If something could be done with that land that helped the Co-op, maybe he would consider letting it go for something other than residential use."

"Oh, wow," Lucy said. "I won't tell anyone we had this talk."

"Thank you," Valentina told her. "It's not exactly a secret mission or anything. And you of all people know that Mr. Radcliffe's heart is always in the right place when it comes to the people of Trinity Falls."

Lucy chuckled in agreement.

Last year, Lucy had held her debut art exhibition, featuring her amazing paintings of local Trinity Falls landmarks. Mr. Radcliffe had shocked everyone in attendance by swooping in at the last minute and personally buying every single painting. It had caused quite a stir when all of the locals were outbid by the mysterious billionaire on the hill, but everyone was pleasantly surprised when he went door to door, delivering them as gifts to the residents as a way to get to know them all better.

"It's complicated," Lucy began. "The local farmers would tell you that more refrigerated shelf space for produce is what we need. But I'm not sure that's true. More space could equate to more sales, or it could result in a lot of spoiled produce if we overstock. It's hard to know."

"Interesting," Valentina said. The store space was probably at least one third produce already, but in a farming town, maybe that didn't feel like much.

"We have all kinds of other things with minimal shelf

space, though," Lucy went on. "The bakery section is small, and we have an area for work from local artisans that seems to be doing well."

Valentina nodded. She had seen all of those things, and tried plenty of them, too.

"I honestly think you should come and visit the store when you have a good amount of time," Lucy said. "Walk around and see what you think. As someone coming in from outside with a mind for business, you might see things we don't."

"I'll do that," Valentina agreed. "Although my instinct is that you and Tom Dudek have been there the longest and your thoughts and concerns are almost definitely where I need to put my attention if I want to come up with anything."

"How did you think of this in the first place?" Lucy asked.

"Well, I've been trying to convince Mr. Radcliffe to think outside the box about this particular land for a while now," Valentina told her. "But specifically looking at ways to help the Co-op was Tanner's idea."

"That was really nice of him to think of the Co-op," Lucy said with a smile. "You picked a great guy there. I don't know you very well yet—but talk about a way to make an amazing impression."

"Oh," Valentina said, feeling awkward. "No, we're not... We're just colleagues, and friends."

"Are you sure about that?" Lucy asked, glancing through the wide opening to the kitchen, where Tanner stood leaning against the counter talking with Ashton.

When he caught Valentina looking, he winked at her, and she felt her whole face go warm.

Lucy was giggling at her before she could even look back.

"Ugh," Valentina said, wishing she could disappear.

"Don't be embarrassed," Lucy told her quietly. "Why don't you just see where it goes? He's a wonderful man, always ready to lend a hand. And Zeke is a great kid."

"He's the best kid," Valentina heard herself say firmly.

Lucy's eyes started dancing, and Valentina wanted to kick herself.

"How's it going?" Tanner's voice boomed as he entered the room, as if she had called him over with her stolen glance.

"Lucy has been so helpful," Valentina said quickly. "I'm going to go to the Co-op just like she suggested, and pay special attention to the areas we talked about. Thank you so much for bringing me, Tanner."

"It was Joe Cassidy's idea," he said, shrugging but looking pleased.

He is a wonderful man, Valentina thought to herself. *Lucy is right.*

"*Valentina, Valentina*," Zeke yelled, running in from the kitchen with the other little boy hot on his heels. "There's a big ham, and mashed potatoes and green beans, and for dessert there's a *cake*."

"Oh, that sounds like a lot for Mrs. Webb," Valentina said. "Lucy and I have a good plan now, so I think I'd better offer a hand."

"She's a natural born Trinity Falls girl," Lucy declared.

"She sure is," Tanner said, smiling down at Valentina with obvious pride in his eyes as she hurried past.

"I'll help too, Valentina," Zeke said excitedly, dashing up to grab her hand. "The kitchen is this way."

She felt an ache in her chest as she let him lead her. This boy, this man, this whole little town—they were all breaking down the defenses she had kept around her heart for so long.

I can't get attached, she reminded herself. *There is no place for me here, not long term. Sooner or later, Mr. Radcliffe will get everything sold off and he'll send me back to the city.*

For the first time, the thought caused her real pain.

14

VALENTINA

Valentina stepped out of the lobby of her apartment and into the village on Saturday morning, immediately wondering where on earth Tanner was going to park today. When she'd looked out the window earlier, things had already been bustling, but now it felt like the whole town was having a great big Christmas block party.

Most of the streets in the village were closed off for the Hometown Holiday celebration, allowing everyone to walk and mingle freely, which they absolutely were doing.

Happy, excited families shopped as they sipped hot chocolate and snacked on holiday baked goods from the tables set up outside the storefronts. Some of the tables and booths were supporting local charities, so Valentina definitely planned to indulge in some decadent treats today.

The snow from the middle of the week had been cleaned from the street and sidewalks, but still made a beautiful backdrop on the yards and grassy areas. Especially the little town amphitheater and the lawn outside the library, where children chased each other among the last of the Christmas trees the fire department was selling.

To her delight, Caroline from the library waved to her and called out her name as she passed on the other side of the street, and two other people she knew from work waved and wished her Merry Christmas.

Valentina headed across to Columbia Avenue, where Tanner stood on the steps of the Co-op, waiting for her.

"You made it," she said, waving to him. "Where's Zeke?"

"*Valentina*," Zeke yelled, before Tanner could answer, darting over from where he'd been playing with a few other kids.

He ran right up to her and hugged her without hesitation, even though he was in front of his friends.

"It's so good to see you," she told him, hugging him back.

"My dad says I should stay with Elton and his mom while you're in the Co-op," he said excitedly. "But when you're done, I can show you everything at the Hometown Holiday celebration, okay?"

"Yes," she told him. "Definitely. I can't wait."

"Me neither," he said.

She watched after him fondly as he ran after his friend, and noticed the mom giving Tanner a quick wave back to let him know Zeke was in good hands.

"Ready?" Tanner asked.

She turned to tell him that she was, but was arrested by the look of real affection in his eyes.

Has he been thinking about me too?

"Yes," she said, willing herself not to blush. "Let's go."

The Co-op was fairly full, in spite of the big event outside. Plenty of people were sitting at the small cafe tables by the big window, looking out at the snowy ground and celebration. Others were grabbing a pair of gloves or a scarf from the shelf where local artisans' wares were displayed.

"Where do we start?" Tanner asked.

"Let's head over to produce," Valentina suggested.

Thankfully, the grocery areas of the store weren't overly crowded. A worker was placing beautiful red and green bell peppers in the refrigerated section of the produce aisle as they arrived. He was a young guy, but he worked with care. She noticed the name *Seth* on his tag.

"Hi," Valentina said with a smile. "Those look delicious."

"Thanks," Seth replied. "Everyone loves them."

"I'll bet not many go to waste," Valentina said carefully.

"No way," Seth said, laughing. "We generally run out after a day or so and people sort of complain."

"The farmer has too many other contracts to give the Co-op enough," Valentina guessed, shaking her head.

"That's actually not it," Seth said, putting down a tomato before leaning against the display to talk. "They're local and they have a greenhouse. They'd love to sell us more. But you can see we just don't have that much shelf space."

"Could you expand into the eating area?" Valentina asked.

"I mean, people love eating here and it's good for our deli," Seth explained. "We have a little more mark-up on prepared deli items, so it helps us cover losses on other things."

"Wow," Valentina said. "There really is a lot going on here."

"Plus, if we added more refrigerator units, we'd have to pay for them and maintain them," he said. "And the power costs a lot too. The tables are cheap compared to the income we get on them. It allows us to keep prices down on staples."

"Seth, you know a lot about how the store works," Valentina said, honestly impressed.

"I'm a member, too," he said, smiling and looking pleased. "And I joined the board last year."

"They're lucky to have you," Valentina told him. "Thanks for talking with me."

"You work for Mr. Radcliffe, right?" Seth asked.

"I sure do," she said. "I'm Valentina."

"Seth," he replied. "Nice to meet you. Your boss is a good guy. I think we all misjudged him a little at first."

"I'll tell him you said so, Seth," she said, offering him her hand to shake before she remembered that she wasn't supposed to do that.

But Seth took her hand and shook it firmly, looking delighted. They moved along and Seth went back to placing peppers on the display.

"That was amazing," Tanner told her.

She thought he might be teasing, but she glanced up

and saw by the look on his face that he was really impressed.

"Well, we got really lucky," she told him. "What are the chances that the guy stocking bell peppers is on the board?"

"Around here?" Tanner asked. "Pretty good, actually. A lot of us are passionate about the Co-op. Having our own grocery store is a big deal in a little town like this."

"You're right," she realized out loud. "My dad always says a job you don't get paid to do is the most rewarding kind. I think I'm starting to finally understand what he was talking about."

"Your dad sounds like a pretty smart guy," Tanner said. "I think I'm going to like him."

She tried her best not to think about how much she wanted to introduce Tanner to her parents, and they continued their slow tour of the store. As Valentina paid attention to which items were stocked and where the empty shelves were, an idea began to form in her mind.

Of course, her brainstorming was interrupted several times as shoppers stopped Tanner to say hello and ask about Zeke and the rest of his family. But she found that she didn't mind a bit. There was nothing nicer than seeing how the people in this little community cared about each other.

When they reached the far rear corner of the store, a bulletin board caught her eye. A simple flyer advertised a variety of outdoor activities, including camping, over at the Williams Homestead.

"Hey," she said to Tanner. "Isn't that your aunt and uncle's place?"

"It is," he told her.

"Caroline tells me about the projects they're doing over there all the time," Valentina said thoughtfully.

"We should definitely go visit," Tanner said. "It's slow going over there right now, but what they've got so far is really wonderful."

"That sounds great," she told him, making the mistake of looking up into his eyes.

There was longing in his gaze now that was impossible to miss. His jaw was tight, like it was taking everything he had not to do whatever it was he wanted to do when he looked at her.

Valentina felt that pull she'd felt the other night all over again—like she was about to fall right into him, her heart pounding loudly enough for them to hear it over at the amphitheater.

"We should probably go find Zeke," Tanner bit out, tearing his gaze from hers. "Before he runs Elton's mom ragged."

"Absolutely," she said, still feeling a little breathless.

She wondered for a second if maybe she was imagining things—mooning over him when he didn't feel the same.

Then she felt the warmth of his hand at the small of her back and her heart flip-flopped in her chest.

What is happening to me?

15

TANNER

Tanner felt an unexpected sense of possessiveness overcome him as he led Valentina out of the store.

He had never known anyone like her, and he'd never felt this way before, like his whole world was shifting and turning itself to make room for her, leaving a yawning emptiness he could feel in his chest every time she looked up at him and he didn't take her in his arms and kiss her the way she needed to be kissed.

They had almost made it down to the street again, where Zeke and Elton were playing with a few more friends, when he spotted a familiar face.

"Mrs. Hastings," he said. "It's nice to see you."

"Hello, Tanner," she said with a smile, as if she hadn't taken to torturing his boy with her mountains of homework.

She honestly seemed too young and friendly to be putting such a burden on little kids.

"*Mrs. Hastings*," Zeke yelled suddenly, tearing up the

street and onto the sidewalk to greet her. "Mrs. Hastings, you came to the celebration."

"Hello, Ezekiel," she said fondly. "I sure did. You children told me how special this was, and I can already see that you're right."

"Zeke," Elton called to him impatiently, and the boy got a torn expression on his face.

"Go on," Mrs. Hastings said. "Don't make your friend wait for you."

"Okay, goodbye, Mrs. Hastings," Zeke squeaked before darting back down to his friend.

"He's such a lovely boy," Mrs. Hastings said, looking after him.

"He really loves you," Tanner told her honestly.

Valentina caught his eyes and raised her eyebrows, as if to tell him to say something.

But what was he supposed to say? You were supposed to treat teachers with respect. He was pretty sure that Aunt Leticia would have been furious if someone had stopped her in the street to complain about her teaching, back when she was a math teacher before his cousins came along.

"Zeke really wants to make you proud by doing his homework every day," Valentina said calmly. "But it sometimes takes him from the minute he gets home until bedtime to finish."

"Oh dear. It shouldn't take that long," Mrs. Hastings said, looking horrified. "That's not what I'm planning for when I assign it."

"How long should the homework take, would you

say?" Valentina asked, still calm, with a thoughtful expression.

"No more than forty-five minutes," Mrs. Hastings said firmly. "Children have to be children. They can't sit at the kitchen table all night."

"Oh wow," Valentina said, nodding. "How about this? Zeke could do his homework for forty-five minutes, and his dad can sit with him to make sure he's working hard the whole time. Then when the timer goes off, maybe Tanner can make a note on the page and sign it. That way you would know for sure that Zeke worked hard, did his best, and put in exactly the amount of time you wanted."

Tanner braced himself. Somehow, the way Valentina said it made the whole thing seem really reasonable. But in his experience, authority figures wanted respect. They didn't want you asking to change the rules. Mrs. Hastings wasn't going to like it one bit.

"I love it," Mrs. Hastings said happily. "Oh, I'm so glad that you brought this up. I know that wasn't easy for you. But I'm grateful you did, and this solution sounds just right for Zeke."

"That's so great," Valentina said with a big smile. "Thank you for stopping to chat about it, especially over the weekend."

Tanner figured he was the only one noticing Valentina's shoulders going down slightly with relief. She *had* been worried, but she had gone to battle for Zeke anyway.

He swallowed over a lump in his throat, wondering why tears were prickling his eyes.

"You know, I may just suggest this strategy to the

other parents as well," Mrs. Hastings said thoughtfully. "I got a few email messages complaining about homework at the beginning of the year, but since second grade is the first year where they get substantial work outside of school, I didn't think it was anything but growing pains."

"That's understandable," Valentina said, nodding.

"I used to teach the fourth grade," Mrs. Hastings confided. "This is my first year with second graders, and the adjustment is a learning curve for me, too. I should have realized."

"The kids love you," Valentina said firmly. "And it's clear how much you care about them. As far as I'm concerned, you're doing an amazing job."

"I'm so glad Zeke has you in his life," Mrs. Hastings said to Valentina with a warm smile, then turned to Tanner. "And of course, you two make such a lovely couple."

Tanner felt a burst of pride and excitement.

"*No*," Valentina said sharply.

There was an awkward pause.

"Oh," Mrs. Hastings said. "I'm sorry."

"We work together and we're friends," Valentina said, her calm, friendly voice back in place again. "But of course, I would never get involved romantically with someone I work with."

Never.

A moment later, Zeke came running back over and Mrs. Hastings said her goodbyes. But Tanner was in a haze the whole time, as the hope that had been slowly growing inside him wilted and died in his chest.

16

VALENTINA

Later that day, Valentina let Joe Cassidy help her into the horse drawn carriage as the afternoon sun began to set over the Hometown Holiday celebration.

"There you go," Joe said with a smile.

"Thank you," she told him.

Zeke scrambled in with Joe's help to snuggle beside her, and Tanner swung his big form up to sit on Zeke's other side.

She couldn't help noticing Tanner was wearing his cowboy hat again. It was worn in just enough that she was starting to think he had actually worn it when he was helping out on neighboring farms, as someone in town had suggested he liked to do. Something about seeing him in it made her feel melty inside, though he wasn't sparing her a glance right now.

Zeke had spent the whole day lit up with happiness, showing Valentina everything the little town's Christmas festival had to offer. They had eaten delicious homemade treats, run between the Christmas trees, played games in the municipal lot, eaten Shirley Ludd's famous chicken and dumpling soup for lunch, taken a ride with Santa Claus on a fire engine, and stopped to say hello to so many kids and their parents that Valentina would never remember them all.

The only thing left to do was the town caroling, which ended with the Christmas tree lighting.

Valentina had been looking forward to the tree lighting ever since she moved into her apartment and realized she had a great view of the tree.

But somehow, she had spent all day today under the shadow of Tanner's silence. He'd been uncharacteristically quiet ever since the end of their chat with Mrs. Hastings, and Valentina wasn't sure why.

Did he not want me getting involved in Zeke's schooling? Did he not like that Mrs. Hastings thought we were together?

A little voice in the back of her head whispered that it might be that he hadn't liked her denying it so vehemently. But if Tanner wanted to date her, surely he would have asked by now. The man had the drive to back up his quiet confidence, and he certainly wasn't a coward.

Besides, as soon as Mrs. Hastings made that assumption out loud, Valentina had known to her bones that she never would feel right seeing someone she worked with anyway. A workplace called for a certain level of professionalism, after all. As the woman Tanner reported to directly, she knew it would be wrong for her to let her foolish heart rule over her conscience.

But now, whenever she let her eyes stray from Zeke to his father, she wished she could just go home, curl up, and have a good cry. She was going to have to get some space from the two of them. But the very idea made her feel empty inside.

Joe clucked to the horses and the carriage lurched to a start. And when Zeke squeaked in surprise and joy, Valentina couldn't help smiling.

The carriage took them down Park Avenue past the pretty little shops and people chatting at the Christmas trees, all the way to Princeton Avenue. It was chilly enough out that Valentina's cheeks were getting cold, but the lap blanket Joe had pulled over them kept them cozy.

Zeke had gotten quiet by the time they reached Princeton. When they turned onto Vassar to head back into the village, he slumped onto her shoulder, completely asleep.

"Oh, wow," she whispered, wrapping an arm around him. "I guess you were pretty worn out."

Tanner made a small sound, and she made the mistake of looking up at him.

He was eyeing his son with a sort of longing that didn't make any sense. It was Valentina who felt pained at the idea of needing to distance herself from them. Tanner would always have Zeke.

His eyes flashed to hers, and a flare of awareness shot through her.

She waited for him to say something, anything.

But Tanner remained silent. The clip-clop of the horses' hooves was the only sound as they rode slowly down the tree-lined street, past the wood-frame Victorians strung with Christmas lights that turned on one by one as the last of the afternoon faded into evening.

When they reached the village again, she turned to Tanner.

"I'm pretty worn out myself," she said quietly. "I think I'll just run home now. Will you tell Zeke I had a great time with him?"

Tanner nodded without looking at her.

Joe Cassidy got down from the carriage and helped her out first.

"Thank you," she told Joe. "You were right. It was wonderful to see the whole town this way."

"My pleasure, sweetheart," Joe said as she stepped onto the sidewalk.

She quickly joined the crowd of people heading down Park Avenue for the tree lighting, not wanting to be there when Tanner got out, ideally with a sleeping Zeke on his shoulder to slow him down.

All the storefronts had their holiday lights blazing now, and the streetlamps cast a warm light over the chattering crowd.

It was strange to be surrounded by so much happiness when it felt like her own heart was breaking. She hurried to her building, her hands shaking a little and making it hard to unlock the main door.

At last, she was in the overheated lobby, tears prickling her eyes.

I just have to make it upstairs. I'll put on my cozy pajamas and a Christmas movie and melt into the sofa.

～

HALF AN HOUR LATER, she had her fleece jammies on and a cup of hot cocoa in her hand. She had meant to put on a movie, but the sound of the whole town singing Christmas carols drew her to the window.

The soft glow of the solar path lights leading to the library allowed her to make out the figures below, smiling and singing around the big tree. There was such peace and happiness on all the faces huddled together against their snowy backdrop.

Without meaning to, she found herself grabbing her phone off the windowsill where it was charging, and calling her parents. Someone picked up on the second ring.

"Hey, Vale," Rafael said. "What are you doing calling on a Saturday night?"

"Hi, Rafe," she said and then was mortified to find herself bursting into tears.

There was a slight click as someone picked up the other extension.

"Hello?" her mother said.

"I've got it, Ma," Rafe told her quickly. "It's for me."

"Okay, be ready for dinner soon," Mama said, hanging up.

"What's going on?" Rafe asked Valentina. "You don't sound so good."

"I'm not so good," she admitted, sniffling and trying to stop crying.

"Who is he?" Rafe demanded playfully. "I'll kill him."

"He's just the *nicest man*," she sobbed.

"Wow," Rafe said. "Then why are you crying?"

"He works for Mr. Radcliffe," she said. "So I can't date him."

"Doesn't half the town work for your boss?" Rafe asked. "Are you just supposed to join a convent or something?"

"He reports directly to me," Valentina said. "Maybe if he were on the paint crew or something it would be different. I could talk to Mr. Radcliffe, but—"

"Talk to him anyway," Rafe said. "He adores you. You know that. He wouldn't want you to give up a good man for him."

"It's not just that," Valentina admitted.

"Oh, here we go," Rafe said. "What else is it?"

"He's got a little boy," Valentina said. "The most incredible little boy."

"Oh," Rafe said, sounding surprised.

"I can't date a man with a child, not in Trinity Falls," she finished miserably. "It wouldn't be fair."

"Why not?" Rafe asked.

"Because I can't stay here," she said. "Not forever. Mr. Radcliffe will close out this project, and honestly there's nothing else for me to do here. He'll send me back to the city, and I really can't do that to Tanner and Zeke."

"Oh," Rafe said sadly.

"And I... I can't stay here," she told him.

"Obviously not," he said right away. "You've spent your whole life following your dreams and working your butt off. You can't give it up to play house with some random guy in the middle of nowhere."

She wanted to argue with him—tell him that Tanner

wasn't some random guy, and that Zeke touched her heart in ways she had a hard time describing.

But all of that paled in comparison to the debt she owed to her parents for the sacrifices they had made for her. She couldn't give it all up now, not when she was so close to securing them the future they deserved.

"Yeah," she said, her eyes on the figures out the window. "They can't go, and I can't stay. It's as simple as that."

The people outside were all gazing up at the big tree, their eyes filled with expectation. The sweet simplicity put an ache in her chest.

"I've gotta go," she told Rafe.

"Call me anytime," he told her. "I'm here for you, even if all I can do is listen."

"Thanks, Rafe," she said. "I love you, big brother."

"Love you too, champ," he told her.

She placed the phone down and leaned closer to the window, watching as the crowd seemed to collectively hold their breath.

Suddenly, the tree was blazing with brilliant light, illuminating the wonder-filled faces of the crowd and casting a dazzling rainbow on the snowy library lawn.

Valentina could just hear the applause and joyful laughter from her window. She longed to be down there too, celebrating the day with the people she cared about.

But those weren't really her people. And she would always be on the outside, looking in, as long as she was here.

17

TANNER

Tanner stood outside one of the homes in the valley with Zeke by his side, looking at his truck and wondering how he had gotten himself into such a jam on Christmas Eve.

The supply house had called him last night to let him know they had finally gotten the right breaker for the panel here. He figured Valentina would be impressed if he got it installed and messaged her to let her know it was ready for inspection photos so far ahead of the scheduled date in mid-January.

Sure, it was Christmas Eve, but it was a quick job, and Zeke liked coming along with his dad for little things like this. After all, their own Christmas Eve tradition mainly consisted of hanging around drinking hot chocolate and Zeke opening a small present before bed.

So, they had trooped over here, and Tanner got the breaker installed quickly, then sent Valentina the simplest message he could:

> #7 is ready for photos of the panel now

> maybe we can do it after Christmas?

After sending it, he'd shoved his phone back in his pocket before he could do something stupid like beg her to see him or talk to him now. He knew it was pathetic to be grasping for reasons to get in touch. She had made it painfully clear how opposed she was to the idea of being with him.

But that didn't change the fact that he missed her terribly.

Even Zeke kept asking about her. And he'd had plenty of time to ask about Valentina, run around with the ball, and even go for a hike during this last week of school, all because she'd had the courage to stand up for him and tell Mrs. Hastings what he needed.

True to her word, Mrs. Hastings had even sent out a message to all the parents, encouraging them to use the same method Valentina had suggested. With a single moment of bravery and genuine caring for Zeke, Valentina had managed to make life better for every child and parent in a whole class of second graders.

That alone made Tanner's heart ache every time he thought about it. How could he just let her get away?

It makes no sense to chase a woman who doesn't want me.

But now, because he was so desperate to talk to her, he had come to work on a holiday, and he must have driven over a nail on the way into the work area. His tire was completely flat. And since he'd loaned his spare to a buddy working the site last week who had done the same thing, he couldn't do anything about it. They were stuck.

"Our truck won't work?" Zeke asked sadly, gazing at the truck that faithfully took him everywhere he'd ever wanted to go.

"It's okay," Tanner told him right away. "It's just the tire. I'm going to call someone to come get us."

He planned to call his cousin, Logan. But his phone started ringing as he was pulling it out of his pocket.

Valentina Jimenez

He slid his thumb across the screen to answer right away.

"Valentina," he said, his voice a little too deep with emotion.

"I, uh, can come take that photo now if you're still there," she said, sounding oddly nervous.

"Sure," he said. "My truck has a flat, so we're stuck here anyway."

"I'll see you in a few minutes," she said, and ended the call.

"*Oh, wow,*" he sighed, running a hand through his hair and blowing out a breath, trying to figure out why she was really coming out, and whether maybe, just maybe she had changed her mind and wanted an excuse to talk to him too. "*Wow...*"

"Was that Valentina?" Zeke asked him. "Why are you being weird?"

"That was Valentina," Tanner told him. "She's coming now."

"To fix the tire?" Zeke asked dubiously.

"No," Tanner said, unable to hide his smile at the idea of Valentina changing a tire. Though he was pretty sure that like anything else in the world, she could definitely do it if she put her mind to it. "She's coming to look at the work I just did. I'll call Uncle Logan about the tire."

"Valentina," Zeke sighed, with the same goofy smile on his face that Tanner was pretty sure he was wearing right now.

"Yup," Tanner told him.

He pulled out his phone and messaged Logan to let him know what was going on.

"She likes your cowboy hat," Zeke said suddenly.

"Huh?" Tanner said.

"You know, your cowboy hat," Zeke said, indicating the truck, where the hat in question was stowed. "She smiles when she looks at it."

He grabbed his hat out of the truck, wondering what his life had come to if he was taking advice on romance and fashion from a seven-year-old. But he wasn't doing so well on his own, and beggars couldn't be choosers.

By the time he had the hat on his head and had messaged back and forth a couple of times with Logan, he heard a car pulling into the driveway.

"Here she comes," Zeke said excitedly as they watched her dark blue sedan pull up.

Tanner felt like he was holding his breath as Valentina got out of the car. She had her usual wool coat on, but he could see she was wearing jeans and brown boots under it, and her long dark hair cascaded down over her shoulders.

We had a good influence on her, he decided. *We got her to let her hair down a little, if nothing else.*

"Hi, guys," she said, waving a little awkwardly.

Sure enough, Zeke was right. Her eyes slid up to

Tanner's cowboy hat as she approached, and her awkward smile deepened into a real one, dimples and all.

"Hey, thanks for coming out on Christmas Eve," Tanner told her.

"I'm sorry about your tire," she said. "Do you have someone coming? If not, I can give you a ride home after this."

"My cousin is on his way," Tanner told her. "But thanks."

"Valentina," Zeke exploded.

She turned to him, her smile brightening when he wrapped his arms around her and gave her a big hug.

"What do you want for Christmas?" Zeke demanded, pulling back and looking up at her so intensely that Tanner thought he was about to start taking notes.

"I have pretty much everything I could want, thank goodness," she told him. "So I always make a wish for my parents to be safe and healthy. And so far, I've gotten exactly what I wanted every single year."

"You don't get any presents at all?" Zeke asked sadly. He was clearly too young to understand what a blessing a parent's good health could be.

"Oh, I *always* get other presents," she told him. "There's supposed to be some bad weather this year, and Mr. Radcliffe has a lot going on, so I'm not traveling to see my family. But they sent me a great big box in the mail, and I'm sure it's full of fun stuff. I can't open it until tomorrow."

"You might be able to figure out what's in there if you shake it," Zeke advised her with a serious expression. "Did you shake it?"

"I might just give that a try when I get home," she told him.

"Okay," Tanner said. "Let's show Valentina the electrical panel so she can get home."

Zeke shot him a look of frustration, but Tanner knew better than to keep Valentina from working when she wanted to work.

They all trooped into the house and down the basement steps to the electrical panel.

Tanner had done some rewiring, but he'd also redone most of the work in the panel. He was proud of how safe and efficient it would be from now on. He had left the face plate off for the photos so Randy would be able to see that there was no longer an ugly tangle of wires behind it.

"I guess I shouldn't send this to Randy until the twenty-sixth," Valentina said sadly, looking down at the image on her screen.

Tanner turned quickly, before she could see him smiling.

"What?" she demanded.

"You would work night and day if you could," he teased her. "Wouldn't you?"

"I like my work," she said lightly.

"How's the presentation for Baz turning out?" he asked her as he held the face plate back up and slid one of the screws in place to tighten it.

"It's almost done," she said, moving to hold the face plate for him, making it much easier for him to place the next screw.

"That's great," he told her, finishing the second screw and moving on to the third one.

"It's missing something though," she said.

"Did you ever get out to the Williams Homestead?" he asked her as he placed the fourth and final screw.

"No," she said softly.

It occurred to Tanner that she probably wasn't comfortable going out there on her own after having to make it so clear that she didn't want to be with him.

"Listen," he told her, lowering his screwdriver and closing the door to the panel cover. "We're friends, and that place belongs to my aunt and uncle. Why don't we run over there now?"

"Isn't a storm coming?" she asked nervously.

"Sure," he said. "But not for hours. And it's not like we're going into the wilderness or anything. The big house is right there, and Logan and Ansel live on the homestead with their families too. There are plenty of places to shelter if we had to."

He had been so careful to say *we're friends*. He hoped it would be enough to make her feel comfortable. He wanted to help her, whether she wanted to be his girl or not. And he would spend any time with her that he could get.

"I did want to talk to Mr. Radcliffe about this before his wedding," she said thoughtfully.

"Well now you'll have time to visit, think about it, and incorporate it into your plan, if there's a way," he told her. "And you can still present everything to him before he goes off on his honeymoon."

"Let's do it," she said excitedly. "But what about your truck?"

"I'll bet Logan and Caroline will take care of it for us," he predicted, knowing his cousin would do whatever he had to do if it meant Tanner getting more time with Valentina.

"We're going to see Great-aunt Annabelle?" Zeke asked.

"We sure are," Tanner told him. "But we're riding with Valentina, so I need to grab your booster and leave the keys for Uncle Logan."

As he ran over to his truck, he willed himself not to see this turn of events as some kind of Christmas miracle. But he couldn't stop his heart from pounding.

18

TANNER

A few minutes later, Tanner stood at the main driveway of the Williams Homestead and smiled as he listened to Zeke explaining who lived there.

"That's the big house," he said, pointing to it. "That's where my great-aunt and uncle live, and over there is where the cabins are."

"Those are for tourists?" Valentina asked him.

"Yes, and for kids from schools," Zeke said. "And past that is Uncle Logan and Aunt Caroline's house, then Uncle Brad and Josie. And then all the way, all the way back, is where Uncle Ansel lives with Lucas, and his new stepmom Aunt Winona, and his new stepsister, Parker."

Tanner tried to hide his smile. Valentina was right, the boy was bright—seeing him dropping hints about stepmothers with a big smile and shining eyes made Tanner wonder just how smart his seven-year-old could be.

"That's so nice that everyone lives together here,"

Valentina said. "Even if they have different houses. My boss, Mr. Radcliffe, and your Aunt Emma will be living here too, right?"

"Yes, in the *castle*," Zeke said excitedly.

"That sounds super cool," Valentina told him. "So where should we go first?"

Zeke looked to his dad.

"I think we'll end with the big house," Tanner said. "I texted my mom that we were coming, and she was super excited because she's got a gingerbread cake in the oven that should be glazed and ready by the time we're done."

"*Yes*," Zeke yelled.

"Why don't we head down to see the cabins and the Native American display," Tanner suggested. "We can see the creek and the trails too, maybe even make it as far as the castle."

"Sounds great," Valentina said.

"Now, it might be faster and more fun to ride," he suggested. "The stables are this way."

"No," Valentina said quickly. "Let's walk. I've been wanting to stretch my legs all day."

"Okay," he said, surprised. He thought everyone loved to ride, especially when it was cold out and you were covering a bit of ground. "Just remember that the horses are available to ride and of course they have lessons here too, if you're noting down what the place has to offer."

"Of course," she said, looking almost relieved.

"Let's head out then," he said.

Zeke took off like a shot, ignoring the path and blazing his own trail through the tall grass.

"Let's slow it down for our guest," Tanner reminded him.

"Sorry, Valentina," Zeke yelled, turning and tearing back across the field for her.

"That's okay," she told him. "I'll do my best to keep up."

The next hour passed in a happy rush of fresh air, conversation, and about a million questions from Valentina.

Tanner did his best to let Zeke answer first, and he was blown away at how much his son had been paying attention when they visited the homestead.

Valentina was especially interested in the small learning center about the Lenni Lenape tribe that once thrived in Pennsylvania. She paused to read each description of what life was like for them before settlers arrived from Europe, and she admired the reproductions of their art and tools.

"You don't see anything like this locally," she said.

"Well, there's a museum in the Poconos," he told her. "It has a big gift shop, and the proceeds support the remaining tribe members. This is just a small display."

"I think it's wonderful," she told him. "And it's nice that it's close to the cabins and easy for people to find."

"Let's go down the path by the creek," Zeke said, his eyes lighting up.

"Okay," Tanner said, lifting his eyes to the gray sky. The storm wasn't supposed to come for another two hours, but the clouds were a little dark for his liking.

But when he glanced down again and saw Valentina

and Zeke looking so excited, he figured they should be okay for a little longer.

"We can go as far as Logan and Caroline's place," he told them. "But then we have to turn back if we want to have time to get back to the big house and still have Valentina home before the storm."

"Okay, Dad," Zeke said.

The two of them took off down the wooded path. Tanner had been roaming these woods and hunting for crawdads in the creek since he was much littler than Zeke, and both he and his son knew just about every inch of the forest.

But Tanner found himself noticing every jagged rock and slippery deposit of leaves now that Valentina was with them. She was handling herself like a pro, and she didn't even seem to be out of breath. But gym workouts didn't really prepare a person for stepping on a rotten log or losing your footing on a muddy hillside.

She'll be fine, he reminded himself. *She can do anything.*

As soon as the thought occurred to him, he heard Zeke yelp.

He looked up, moving as he did, expecting to see Valentina in trouble.

Instead, Zeke was sliding down the muddy bank toward the creek. He had probably been too busy regaling Valentina with tales of their adventures in the woods to be cautious, and now, if Tanner was lucky, he would simply get wet and banged up a little.

Please don't let his precious head hit a rock, he prayed as he sprinted for them.

But before he could get to the boy, Valentina was

moving. She bolted down the slippery bank and grabbed Zeke, dragging him back up, even as her right leg gave out under her.

"Whoa," Zeke gasped, crouching on stable ground. "Are you okay, Valentina?"

"I'm fine," she said quickly, dragging herself back up and sitting in the path. But Tanner could tell by her pallid skin and glassy-eyed gaze that she wasn't.

"You saved me, Valentina," Zeke said, his voice full of wonder. "I could have bumped my head and drowned."

Tanner moved beside her, thinking to himself that at least the boy had listened to some part of what he's said when he warned him about venturing too close to the slippery bank.

"You rolled your ankle, didn't you?" Tanner asked her gently.

"I think so," she said, nodding.

Tanner knew that hurt. He'd done it himself back in high school when he played football.

"Here's what we're going to do," he said. "Zeke is going to *carefully* find me a stick. And we're going to make you a little splint to stabilize it. Okay?"

"Okay," she agreed.

"Then we'll just head back," he told her. "I can carry you."

"No, no," she put in.

"Well, you can lean on me," he told her. "And we'll be just fine."

Something cold and wet fell on his cheek. He moved to wipe it away, but before he could, the sound of a million tiny taps surrounded them.

"It's ice," Valentina said, brushing the frozen rain from her forehead. "The storm…"

"We'll be fine," he told her again.

"Found a stick, Dad," Zeke said happily, darting back to them looking like he didn't have a care in the world."

"Perfect," Tanner told him, pulling off his coat. "Hold this for me."

He laid it over Valentina, hoping it would protect her from the ice a bit. Then he pulled off his flannel too, and ripped one of the sleeves off it.

"Oh, no," Valentina said softly. "Your shirt."

"It's fine," he told her. "I have a million of these."

He worked quickly to secure her ankle, breaking the stick in two and putting one on each side before binding the whole thing tightly with his sleeve.

Zeke was by her side again, holding her hand.

She set her jaw and refused to make a single sound of pain, though he knew from experience it had to be agony when he moved her foot around before tightening the material.

"There you go, Valentina," Zeke said comfortingly. "All set. You were so brave."

"Thank you," she told him with a genuine smile. "Thank you for holding my hand."

"It's really coming down," Tanner realized out loud as he pulled his coat back on. "We should try to go now."

"I'll be fine," Valentina said.

But when he lifted her to her feet she gasped, and he could practically hear the scream she wanted to let out echoing in the woods.

"I'm cold," Zeke said plaintively.

"Let's go back to the cabins," Tanner decided. "I'm going to carry you, Valentina. It'll still hurt when I move, but we'll get there faster."

She nodded, looking like it was killing her pride to accept his help. But he was glad she didn't argue. He wasn't sure how long it would be safe to be out walking.

He scooped her up, cradling her in his arms. She managed not to make a sound, but he could tell by the way she tucked her face into his neck that she was trying not to whimper.

"Here we go," he said cheerfully, determined not to notice how good she felt in his arms.

She's hurt, he admonished himself. *And you have to focus on getting back to the cabins.*

Fortunately, when they were looking around, he had noticed the middle cabin was stocked with firewood, food, and water. Maybe a camper was expected during the holidays. He had no idea, but he was grateful for it. Hopefully, they could hole up until the worst of the storm was over, and then he could go for help.

The trip back through the woods to the cabins seemed so much longer now that they were contending with wind and ice. Zeke held onto Tanner's coat without being asked, so at least he knew they were all together.

But visibility was fading quickly, and he led them the last fifteen minutes or so mostly on memory. Just when he was starting to worry that he wasn't going in the right direction after all, the first cabin came into view.

"When we get to the middle one," Tanner said to Zeke, "I want you to open the door for us. Okay?"

"Yes, Daddy," Zeke said, his voice brave and loud against the storm.

"Good boy," Tanner told him. "You doing okay, Valentina?"

She nodded against his neck, not making a sound. Zeke let go of his coat when they got to the right cabin, and opened the door.

"Okay," Tanner said in the most comforting way he knew how. "I'm going to lower you down onto the bed, Valentina."

She nodded again and allowed him to slowly place her on one of the little cots.

"Is that okay?" he asked her.

"Yes," she said, giving him a small smile. "I'm embarrassed you had to carry me. But thank you."

Her eyes seemed almost dreamy as she looked up at him, and he swore a current passed between them for a moment.

"It was nothing," he said, looking away as he felt the now-familiar tug, telling him to hold her and never let her go. He wanted to help her, protect her, and be there for her in any way she would allow.

"I guess I should try to get these off," she murmured.

She started trying to remove her boots, and Tanner bent to help her.

"Daddy," Zeke said softly from across the room.

Tanner turned to see tears in the boy's eyes.

"That was scary, wasn't it?" Tanner asked, moving to him and crouching down.

Zeke nodded up and down.

As the icy rain lashed the windows, Tanner realized it might be scary for Zeke now too.

"But we're safe inside," Tanner told him. "Mr. Esh built this cabin, so we know it's extra strong, right?"

"Right," Zeke said bravely.

"I'm going to make a fire so we can all get nice and warmed up," Tanner told him. "Can you keep Valentina company for me? We want to make sure she's not thinking about her hurt ankle."

"Yes," Zeke said, looking thrilled to be assigned such an important task as he scampered over to her bedside.

"Do you want me to tell you a story, Valentina?" he asked her softly.

"Yes, please," she said. "If you want, you can sit with me, too."

"Okay," he said.

She shrugged off her coat and carefully scooted over on the cot.

"Why don't you take off your coat and shoes too?" Tanner offered. "I'll bring you guys a couple of blankets."

He tried not to hover too much as Zeke carefully climbed in, making sure not to hurt Valentina's ankle. Then he put a blanket around Zeke's shoulders and laid another over Valentina.

"Thank you," she mouthed to him.

He nodded and tore his eyes away from her, heading back over to start a fire in the wood stove as Zeke began to murmur a favorite bedtime story to Valentina.

Before too long, Tanner had a nice fire crackling merrily away. The cabin was small, so he knew it would be nice and warm in here in no time.

He searched the cupboards for the right thing to feed everyone. There were cans of soup and baked beans, and packets of cookies as well as oatmeal. He smiled when he saw there was even a box of graham crackers, a bag of marshmallows, and a chocolate bar.

Deciding to save the s'mores ingredients as a surprise, he turned to ask the others if they wanted baked beans or soup.

But the two of them were curled up together, fast asleep.

Tanner found himself moving closer to look down at them, his heart aching.

Zeke had his back to Valentina's chest and her arms were wrapped around him. Their cocoon of blankets looked incredibly cozy, but it was the expression of happiness on both their faces, even in sleep, that tugged at Tanner's heart.

This didn't look like his son with Tanner's work friend, or even with his girlfriend. There was something about the scene before him that made him think of a mother and child.

He knew he should prepare a meal before it was fully dark, plus find back-up batteries for the flashlight on the counter, and be sure the cabin was secure from the storm.

But for some reason, the slow, sweet melody of "Silent Night" filled his mind, and he stayed where he was for a moment, listening to the icy rain outside and watching his two favorite people cuddled together, safe and warm.

Why can't things be different, Valentina? Why can't you be ours forever?

19

TANNER

Tanner sat in the guest room of his aunt and uncle's house early on Christmas morning, sipping hot chocolate with Zeke while Valentina showered in the next room.

Valentina had insisted that Zeke get a warm shower first. He did, and was dressed in a pair of too-big pajamas now. Thankfully, Aunt Annabelle kept spare clothing in all sizes in the big guest room bureau. He seemed awfully happy for a kid whose Christmas presents were all back at the apartment in the village.

On the other hand, Tanner was feeling very happy himself that he'd been able to get the two of them safely up to the big house from the cabins. He'd ventured out into the icy landscape just before the sun came up and found that sure enough, his uncle left the keys on the seat of his old truck.

He'd figured no one would mind him borrowing the truck to run down to the cabins and back. The path was slippery, but the chains were on the truck's tires, and he took it nice and slow.

By the time the sun peeked out over the trees, he could see that the whole homestead was covered in a beautiful layer of ice. It sparkled and twinkled like diamonds, lighting up the fields and making it seem later in the morning than it was.

Valentina and Zeke had been enchanted by the magical sight on the drive back up to the big house. They had even decided to sing "Winter Wonderland" together. Neither of them was particularly good at singing, but that made it almost better, and even Tanner had joined in by the time the truck was climbing the main drive.

He looked down at his son now, marveling at how resilient the boy was. He'd been scared last night. But all day today, he'd been radiant with joy.

"Merry Christmas," Tanner told Zeke softly, ruffling his light brown hair. "I'm sorry we'll have to wait on presents. But it will be so nice to see family right away this year."

"We already got our Christmas miracle," Zeke told him happily.

"Yes, it's so good we made it safely through the storm," Tanner said, nodding.

"Oh yeah," Zeke said. "That too."

"What were you talking about?" Tanner asked.

Zeke's eyes went to the bathroom door, where a tiny wisp of shower steam slipped out from beneath. When they stopped talking, they could just hear Valentina softly singing "Silent Night," the same song that had been playing in Tanner's head last night when he watched her sleeping with Zeke in her arms.

"I got my stepmom," Zeke said dreamily.

Tanner closed his eyes, praying for the strength to talk honestly to his boy without breaking his heart beyond repair.

"She stayed with us," Zeke went on. "And she told me this morning she hadn't slept that well in forever."

"It was really nice to spend time with her," Tanner agreed. "But Valentina's family is in the city. When her job here in Trinity Falls is done, she'll want to go back there to be near her parents and her brothers."

Zeke blinked at him then shook his head.

"She's a good, good friend," Tanner said, before the boy could argue. "And I know she'll miss you a lot when she goes back home."

He had a whole speech forming in his mind. But Zeke suddenly snaked his arms around Tanner's waist and collapsed into his chest, melting into him like he had as a despondent toddler.

Does she really need to go? Shouldn't I ask her to stay?

But there were about a million things wrong with that. The first one being that they weren't even dating. And she had stated pretty clearly that she would never date someone she worked with.

He had thought about simply quitting to remove that obstacle many times since that moment.

But if he left the job just so that they could date, it would throw her timeline into chaos on the Radcliffe land project. And he knew completing that project successfully meant the world to her. She had worked a lifetime to climb that mountain. He couldn't put that in jeopardy for his own selfish reasons.

And besides, what if the work thing was just an excuse, and she really wasn't interested?

But the way she looked at me last night, like I was the most important man in the universe...

There was a tap on the door.

"Come in," Tanner called out softly.

The door opened and Uncle Alistair poked his head inside, his face breaking into a big smile when he saw who it was.

"I thought I heard three little mice sneaking into my house this morning," he said.

"We were stuck in the forest, Great-uncle Alistair," Zeke said, lifting his head from Tanner's chest. "We stayed in a cabin."

"You did?" Alistair looked horrified.

"It worked out just fine, thanks to your stocked cabin," Tanner told him right away. "And I'll restock firewood for you tomorrow."

"Thank goodness you thought of the cabins," his uncle replied, his face suddenly serious. "Why didn't you call us for help?"

"It was Christmas Eve," Tanner said, shrugging. "Besides, it wouldn't have been safe for you to come down in the storm. And now we get to help out with Christmas things a little earlier than usual, right, Zeke?"

"Will Great-aunt Annabelle make gingerbread pancakes?" Zeke asked right away. "And can I flip them?"

"I'll bet she would love to do that with you," Alistair

said with a big smile. "How's your girl holding up after a night of unintended camping?"

He glanced over at the bathroom door, but Tanner shook his head once from behind Zeke.

"She's fine," Tanner said lightly. "She rolled her ankle a little last night, but it seems like she's feeling better today."

"She's a nice lady," Alistair said quickly. "It's good to have good friends. We'll find her some ibuprofen."

"She saved me when I almost fell," Zeke said. "But I made her forget her hurt ankle with a good story."

"You're a good boy, Ezekiel Williams," Alistair declared. "When you're ready, come on down and we'll see about those pancakes. I know your great-aunt's recipe by heart, you know. Maybe we could surprise her."

Zeke squeaked with delight and sprung off the bed to join his great-uncle.

Tanner took one last longing look at the bathroom door and then moved to join them. There was no point sitting here mooning over a woman who didn't feel the same way.

20

VALENTINA

Valentina ventured down the stairs of the big house, feeling a little bit like she was having a *walk of shame* even though she and Tanner weren't even seeing each other, and they had slept in separate cots last night.

But Zeke slept in my cot.

Valentina's heart warmed at the memory of the funny little boy falling asleep trying to whisper stories to her. She had thought maybe it would be tough to share the small cot with a wiggly little one, especially in a cabin with icy wind lashing at the windows. But she honestly hadn't slept that well in a long time.

She paused on the landing, feeling weird again about being at the homestead on Christmas morning.

But laughter and happy chatter floated up the staircase, beckoning her. And she reminded herself how Emma and Mr. Radcliffe had invited her here today, and last Christmas too. She hadn't felt it was right to take them up on it, but at least she had an invitation.

"Valentina," Zeke sang out as she stepped into the kitchen. "I'm making *gingerbread* pancakes."

"Wow, Zeke," she said, feeling instantly at home. "So *that's* the unbelievably delicious smell that made my belly grumble on the way down the stairs."

The boy laughed and glanced up at his great-uncle. The two of them were at the stove together, wearing Christmas aprons with Zeke standing on a step stool to help him reach. Tanner leaned against the counter watching, a cup of steaming coffee in his hands.

"Hey," he said, his deep voice sending a tingle through her. "Come get some coffee."

The rest of the early morning melted by in no time. Mrs. Williams wandered downstairs and exclaimed over the pancakes, which clearly tickled Zeke. More family rolled in, including Mr. Radcliffe and his son, Wes, and Emma, and they all ate and drank fragrant coffee and listened to Zeke regale them with tales from the night before and their adventure in the ice storm.

"Valentina *saved* me," he kept saying. "I was going to fall right into the water, but she swooped me up."

"That was very brave of her," Tanner's aunt said, giving Valentina a warm smile that Valentina felt all the way down to her toes.

"That's how she hurt her ankle," Zeke said, shaking his head sadly.

"Yes, but my ankle will be all better in no time," she told him. "You're irreplaceable."

She helped to clear the table, and was just starting on dishes with Alistair when Mr. Radcliffe came in.

"So, I hear you've been working on something for me," he said, arching a brow.

"Yes," she told him. "Maybe we can talk about it tomorrow."

"Nonsense," he told her. "We're both here now. Let's talk when you're done."

"She's done," Alistair said fondly. "Guests aren't supposed to do all this cleanup anyway."

"You're okay with the rest?" Valentina asked, looking at the sink full of dishes.

"Absolutely," he said, winking at her. "Go talk to your boss."

"Let's go sit in the den," Radcliffe suggested. "It'll be quieter in there."

Sure enough, the rest of the family was gathering in the living room, admiring the tree and teasing the kids about how many presents were under it.

"They're amazing, right?" Radcliffe asked as he sat on the sofa.

It took Valentina a moment to realize what he meant. But of course he was talking about the Williams family.

"You're so lucky," she told him honestly. "They're really special people."

He nodded with a secret smile, though she had no idea what there was to keep a secret about.

"I've got some slides on my phone," she told him. "If you want, we can ask if someone has a laptop I can borrow. Or I can just send them to you. I honestly don't think you need all that for us to have this conversation."

"Fine," Radcliffe said, leaning back and crossing one ankle over his knee. "Hit me."

"The land near where the highway is going in is hard to sell," she said, telling him again what he already knew.

He frowned and she knew it was because he was anticipating her asking him to sell the land commercially, which he'd made it clear that he didn't want to do. But he didn't interrupt this time.

"No one wants to build when there are plenty of nice farmhouses they can move into that are closer to the village and further from where that big road will be," she went on. "So, I've been exploring town, canvassing people, and trying to figure out what's missing."

Radcliffe nodded to her, but he didn't show a lot of enthusiasm.

"You bought up so much of this town because you wanted to save it from being developed and turned into shopping malls and big box stores," she said. "And you did that because you love the town."

He nodded again, looking more interested.

"You love the town because you love the people," she went on. "And you wanted to help them. With that land, you now have a chance not just to save them from bad development, but to offer them *good* development—things the town didn't have before, but really needs."

She cleared her throat and willed herself to be brave. She hadn't gotten where she was by pushing back against Radcliffe when he put his foot down about something.

But this was important, too important to protect her good relationship with her boss and mentor. A month ago, she couldn't have done this. But Tanner had helped her to know the town better. And now that she saw what its people needed, she couldn't sit back if there was something she could do.

"Before I attended a single event in town, I went to the library and read back issues of the paper," she told him. "The Gazette had listings about all the wonderful community events, for weeks in advance of each one. But I could see in the articles that came afterward, that these beloved events are regularly canceled or rescheduled because of rain or snow. Although they look like they're just for fun, these kinds of celebrations are key for community building. And attending a few of them has shown me that many of our small business owners really rely on them to sell their wares. Restaurants expect to serve the crowds. And nearly as many charitable causes as small businesses were represented at the booths for the Hometown Holiday celebration. Missing one of these events due to weather can really make or break a small operation."

Radcliffe leaned forward now, looking much more involved.

"I also visited Cassidy Farm and the Williams Homestead," she went on. "While I'm told that Cassidy Farm has always done well for itself, the Williams Homestead has only recently opened for tourists. They need more business to supplement their grants."

Radcliffe nodded thoughtfully.

"And at the Co-op, there's not enough room for all the produce our local farmers would like to sell," she continued. "Purchasing and running more refrigerators would cut into their already thin margins, so it's just not an option."

"So, what did you have in mind?" Radcliffe asked.

"For starters, we need a large, covered structure," she said. "Like an open market where events can be held on rainy days, and where the farmers can sell produce directly."

"We already have a farmer's market in town," Radcliffe said.

"Not in the winter," Valentina said. "And never when it rains. And it only draws locals. What if it were up by the highway, where people traveling through could stop in and buy healthy food and local crafts? That's another thing they don't have enough space for at the Co-op or even the Christmas shop at Cassidy Farm."

"I see," he said.

"We could also have a little mini-Trinity Falls museum," she went on, unable to hide her smile at one of her latest ideas. "We could have information about the Lenni Lenape tribe, and the founding families—maybe even a miniature Cassidy Farm, and a tourism kiosk with info about the homestead and the other attractions."

"You came up with all of this?" he asked.

She nodded, feeling incredibly proud.

"It's a remarkable idea," he said, shaking his head.

"It would occupy a nice amount of land, but it wouldn't put the project in the black," she told him firmly, swallowing back her own sadness. "And what you would have to sell it for wouldn't be enough for that anyway. I have all the projections in my slides."

Realizing that using the land this way would practically guarantee that her first big project came out as a net loss would have been a tough pill to swallow a month ago. But right now, having spent time with this town and fallen in love with its people, she was ready to make that sacrifice.

"I see," he said.

"You would probably have to lease the land at first, honestly," she told him. "But I know there are local merchants who would pool together to do this. Maybe the borough would even participate. I'm sure that over time they could pay you, and you could get back what you put into it. And you would be giving the town something priceless."

"Valentina," he said, leaning forward again and meeting her eyes. "I'm impressed by what you've done. This goes beyond any other project you've ever mocked up for me. And I'm grateful to you for your work."

"Thank you," she said nervously, unable to help smiling as her heart pounded.

"But my answer is still no," he said briskly, standing.

"What?" she breathed, praying she hadn't heard him right.

"No," he said again, brushing his hands on his pants as if he were clearing himself off the idea. "I'm not going to do that."

He left the room and she stared at the sofa where he had just been sitting, wondering if she had somehow dreamed it all.

Radcliffe would often reject her ideas, that was an everyday thing. But normally he would bat them back and forth with her first, using the opportunity to help her think critically from another perspective until she understood why he had refused, and whether there was a better way to do what she was proposing.

Surely, he could see that this hadn't just been another idea to improve profits or speed up timelines—that it really meant something to her. But he had said no and washed his hands of it without another word.

She rose and moved through the house, still lost in her own thoughts among the sounds of the family laughing and talking all around her.

"We salted the drive," Logan yelled out as he came in the front door with Ansel behind him. "They're saying the roads are cleared now, so the others should be here any minute."

"Oh, thank goodness for you boys," Annabelle said.

Before she knew what she was doing, Valentina grabbed her coat from the hook and bolted out the front door for her car.

It was still freezing outside, but the sun was up, and the homestead glittered like it was covered in diamonds. The cheerful vista was completely at odds with her bitter disappointment.

"Valentina," Tanner called after her. His voice was worried, and when she turned she could see the furrow in his brow. "What's wrong?"

"Nothing," she said quickly, afraid she would cry if she tried to explain what had just happened with Radcliffe, especially after all Tanner and Zeke had done to help her research. "I just have to get home for the family Christmas video-call. I don't want to miss it."

"Of course," he said, looking bitterly disappointed. "Are you sure there's nothing else?"

"I...I guess I just need some space," she said weakly. "Tell Zeke I said Merry Christmas again?"

He nodded, his lips pressed together in a thin line, as if he were trying hard not to say something else.

Once she was safely in the car, she took a deep breath, willing herself not to cry until she was home. This was going to be a rough drive, and she had to take it slowly and calmly.

When she was feeling calm enough, she turned the key, thankful that the engine turned right over. With a heavy heart, she carefully made her way down the drive and headed back toward the village with one thought rising above the rest.

Maybe it really is time to move on...

21

VALENTINA

A week later, Valentina stood in the high field of the Williams Estate, wearing her beautiful bridesmaid dress, and staring at the big brown horse she was supposed to be climbing onto.

The horse stared back at her, looking bored, which somehow made the idea of approaching it all the more terrifying.

The two of them were utterly alone.

In fairness, she had been supposed to get on the horse ten minutes ago when the other bridesmaids did, and warm him up walking and trotting along one of the trails before all meeting up together in the low field, so they could gallop into the wedding together.

She had encouraged the others to go along while she stretched her ankle, even though her ankle was feeling just fine. They had all swung up onto their horses and rode away like it was nothing.

Valentina was heartbroken to realize that in all the excitement and sorrow over her project for Radcliffe, and the confusion over her feelings for Tanner and Zeke, she had let herself forget about getting herself ready to hop on a horse today.

Valentina had never been the kind of person to procrastinate or be in denial. But it was clear to her as she stood in the wintry field, gazing at the beautiful, terrifyingly large animal, that she had lost herself.

Who am I without career success? I've lost my boss's confidence, turned my back on the man I care about, and I'm about to lose my only real friend in Trinity Falls.

Emma had always been kind to her. How was it going to look when the other bridesmaids appeared, and Valentina was just *missing*?

Why do I keep letting my pride get in my way?

She still couldn't believe that in the heat of the moment on Christmas morning she had told Tanner that she needed space.

To his credit, he had given it to her. She hadn't seen him or heard from him since.

At the wedding today, she would have to face him again. It gutted her to imagine what it would be like to spend time with him here, and professionally at work, knowing that he'd let go of her friendship so easily.

But she had a more immediate problem literally staring her in the face.

I can do this, she told herself. *I can do anything.*

But when she approached the big animal, he snorted and tossed his mane, pawing the ground a little, and she found herself backing up again.

"What are we supposed to do?" she asked the horse

quietly, wishing she could negotiate with it, like she did when she hit a wall at work with someone.

"You've never ridden before, have you?" a familiar deep voice asked.

She turned to see Tanner standing there, looking incredibly handsome in a suit with a woolen coat, smiling at her from under his trusty cowboy hat.

"I haven't," she admitted, gulping.

"And the others didn't take time to teach you?" he asked, sounding annoyed.

"I told them I could ride," she admitted, looking at her feet. "It's not their fault."

"You just assumed you could, didn't you?" he asked.

"I did," she said, looking up.

"It's a fair assumption," he said, chuckling. "I think you could do just about anything you put your mind to."

She looked up at him, melting at his gentle gaze.

"I could teach you, but we don't have a lot of time for a lesson," he went on. "So I think we'll just ride together."

"Thank you," she told him, relieved.

"I'm going to hold him while you mount," he told her, heading for the horse. "Then I'll get on behind you."

She noticed that the horse snorted again, tossing his head up and down slightly as Tanner approached.

"Why is he doing that?" she asked nervously.

"He's excited for you to ride," Tanner explained. "He's telling us he's ready to get some exercise."

"Oh," Valentina said, feeling silly. It actually made a lot of sense. After all, the horse had been standing here with her, looking perfectly friendly the whole time.

Tanner showed her how to put her foot in the stirrup

and swing herself up. Though the horse moved around a bit, she was able to get onto his back on her second try.

It felt good, but she was up so high, with nothing around her for support. It made her heart pound.

But a moment later, Tanner was swinging himself up behind her, wrapping his arms around her waist to take the reins, and that all melted away.

She drank in the sensation of safety and warmth. She had daydreamed about having Tanner's arms around her so many times, but she had never imagined how right it would feel.

"Okay," he said, clearing his throat. "We'll take it slow."

He clucked to the horse, and immediately they were moving forward.

She marveled at the feeling of each step the big creature took. There was so much power coiled in his muscles. He could have torn across the field, leaping fences and disappearing into the forest if he wanted. Yet his ears were swiveled back, making it clear that he was eager to take direction from Tanner.

"Here we go," Tanner said.

She could feel him squeezing his thighs around the horse's belly, and then they were moving a little faster. At first, she felt herself being jostled and panicked that she was going to fall off.

"We won't go faster than this," Tanner told her quietly, giving her a gentle squeeze. "Not until it's time to go down the aisle.

Then her heart was beating even harder, not out of fear, but from the awareness of his lips near her hair and his embrace, and the rest of the world ceased to matter for a little while.

"When we take it up to a gallop, it will actually be less bumpy," he told her as they rode under a canopy of bare trees. "Even though we'll be going faster. His gait will make it smoother."

"Okay," she said. "I can handle it."

She was already getting used to the rhythm and the sound of the horse's hooves clomping on the frosty ground.

"How did you know to come for me?" she asked after a moment.

"Natalie came to find me when you didn't show up with the others," he told her. "She was worried about your ankle."

"Oh," she said, surprised and grateful that Natalie had thought to send Tanner.

"You've got some good friends around here," he told her gruffly.

"I guess I do," she realized.

"As soon as I thought about it for a second, I remembered how quickly you refused the chance to ride a horse here on Christmas Eve," he added with a smile in his voice.

She nodded. Looking back, that probably had been suspicious.

"So, when are you going to talk to Baz?" he asked.

"I did," she told him, wanting to run from this conversation, but with nowhere to go. She had known he would ask, and he had a right to hear how it went, after helping her so much. "He said no."

"He *what?*" Tanner sounded completely surprised and horrified. "Why?"

Somehow Tanner being so upset on her behalf made her tear up a little.

"He didn't really say," she said, trying not to give way to her tears. "He just said *no*. But all along he's told me that he won't let go of that land for commercial purposes, so I shouldn't have been surprised. I knew it was a long shot, but I had to try."

"Unbelievable," Tanner muttered.

"It's his land," Valentina said. "And it's his money, and his decision. I can rest easier knowing I tried to show him a viable option that would help the village."

But it was harder to swallow than she let on.

"Here we come," Tanner said as they trotted up a little hillside and spotted the wedding party and guests on the lawn in front of the castle. The other bridesmaids were on horseback in the little valley just below the lawn. "Are you ready to go faster?"

"Yes," she told him, signaling to Natalie.

Natalie gave her horse a little kick and then she was rocketing up the hillside, followed by Caroline, Winona, and Melody. Their hair and dresses billowed as they flew toward the wedding.

"Lean forward on his neck," Tanner murmured.

She did as she was told and then Tanner was squeezing the big brown horse's belly, giving him a tap, and Valentina felt the stallion leap forward.

Just like Tanner said would happen, the horse's gait was more fluid now. Valentina felt like she was flying as they followed the other four women up the hillside and across the lawn to a squealing and delighted Emma.

Emma looked so utterly beautiful and happy in her pretty wedding dress, and Radcliffe looked proud enough to burst, his eyes on her as she clapped and waved to her friends.

"Great job," Tanner murmured in Valentina's ear, distracting her from the strange emotion she felt watching her friend. "I'll get off and then help you down."

Tanner leapt from the horse with the grace of a dancer, and Valentina tried and failed to do the same, letting him catch her in his arms and help her get her feet on the ground.

Though the other bridesmaids held their horses' reins as they lined up beside Emma, Valentina was grateful when Tanner led her mount away. She had actually enjoyed the ride a lot, but she still wasn't sure about trying to tell the big beast what to do herself.

I did ride him though, Abuelo, she told her grandfather silently, wondering what he would have made of her needing so much help.

Then the ceremony began, and Valentina was lost in the sweetness of the intimate event. By the end, she found herself weeping with joy as the beautiful words were exchanged.

22

VALENTINA

Valentina headed into the wedding reception feeling joyful and excited.

Emma had been beyond thrilled at the sight of her bridesmaids riding in on horseback, just like the sisters in *The Princess and the Stable Boy*. Between that and her obvious joy at being married after a year of waiting, the atmosphere in the bedroom where the girls all huddled to touch up their hair and lipstick and rehash the ceremony was beyond joyful.

Now they were all climbing the steps to the ballroom together. And Valentina couldn't help the happy anticipation she felt at the idea of seeing Tanner.

We're just friends, she tried to tell herself. But it was getting harder and harder to believe it.

At last, she followed Emma and the others through the big wooden doors and into the ballroom.

The floors were black and white checkerboard, just like in the foyer below. But that was where the similarities ended.

Huge windows went from waist-height all the way up to the two-story ceiling, each surrounded by what had to be a foot and a half of beautiful original moldings, with a gorgeous vista of sky and trees. Three big crystal chandeliers sparkled above, and a group of familiar men and women played an acoustic guitar cover of "Here Comes the Sun" as Emma walked in.

"Oh, wow," Caroline sighed at the sight of it, and Valentina couldn't think of a better reaction.

But her excitement was cut short when she looked to the other side of the ballroom. Guests were just beginning to arrive, but Radcliffe was already there, talking tensely in the corner with an angry-looking Tanner. Valentina headed over automatically, worry in her heart.

"You say you love this town," Tanner was saying, loudly enough for everyone to hear. "But you won't even listen to the person who is in the best position to know what it needs?"

"I'm not going to have this argument with you, Tanner," Radcliffe said calmly.

"So you want to do good for this town, but only when you're the one who gets all the credit?" Tanner asked.

A murmur went through the room.

"Tanner," Valentina said softly, hurrying over. "This isn't a good time."

"Is there ever a good time for a man to take advantage of a woman's good character and years of hard work?" Tanner demanded, turning back to Radcliffe. "Treating her like a secretary when she should be a CEO?"

"Tanner, that's not fair to Mr. Radcliffe," she said.

"She deserves better, Baz," Tanner said. "And you know it."

By now the rest of the ballroom had gone silent. And Valentina's cheeks burned as tears prickled at her eyes.

"You're right," Radcliffe said suddenly. "Valentina, you're fired."

There were gasps and whispers of horror.

"I-I'm sorry—" she stammered as Tanner looked on with panic in his eyes.

"No," he said. "This has been a long time coming. And I wasn't going to do this today, but I guess like Tanner says, there's no time like the present. Come with me, please, Valentina—just you."

Head down, she followed him through the ballroom, and into a much more modest room with a desk and two chairs.

"This is going to be my office when we move in," he said after closing the door, his voice softer now and strangely friendly, given the circumstances. "It used to be where the servants waited for someone to ring them, when they were needed."

It might be a while before someone needs me again, she thought to herself darkly.

"I have good news and bad news for you, Valentina," Radcliffe said, seating himself and gesturing for her to take the chair opposite his.

She seated herself, wondering what could possibly be considered good about her current situation.

"I was going to wait until after the wedding to tell you," he said. "I wanted it to be a little more formal. But that hot-headed admirer of yours forced my hand."

"I'm sorry," she said quietly.

"The truth is, I've already sold that land without restriction to a corporation," he said. "And I cleared enough on it that the whole project is in the black."

It was the opposite of what he said he wanted, but at least she would be leaving with a successful project on her resumé. That was the good news. What it meant for the town was another story...

"I thought you weren't going to sell to anyone who needed commercial zoning," she said.

"I trust this buyer," he told her. "And I know they won't do anything with the land that I wouldn't do. They're already invested in the community."

The only person in Trinity Falls Valentina knew of who had that kind of wealth, besides Mr. Radcliffe himself, was the tech genius who was new to town, Angel's brother.

"Julian," she said thoughtfully, wondering what the man would do with all that land when he already had another community project going.

"Not Julian," Mr. Radcliffe said, shaking his head.

"Forgive me, sir," she said. "But I think there are only two people in Trinity Falls with those kind of resources."

"Now there are three," Radcliffe said simply, pulling an envelope from the desk drawer and handing it to her.

She gazed at him, wondering what on earth was going on.

"Go on," he said. "Open it."

She opened the envelope, pulling out several pieces of paper and studying them for a moment. They catalogued a large land sale to a company called The Valentine Corporation at a price that seemed more than fair.

"I don't understand," she said at last. "These are deeds."

"And your letter of resignation, and a document of incorporation," Radcliffe said. "The deeds won't mean anything until we both sign them in front of a notary, but Sloane Greenfield is here today. I'm sure she'll help us out if you don't want to wait."

"Why would I sign them?" Valentina asked.

"Because I just fired you," Radcliffe told her. "And this is your severance package. The land is yours to do with whatever you want. And you can rename your corporation, if you'd like."

"So, you bought it... from yourself?" she asked. "To give to me?"

"Something like that, yes," he said with a smile.

"What if I didn't want it?" she asked, still too gobsmacked to take in what was happening.

"Then I'll keep it," he told her. "And you can have your package in cash instead. I've told you I'm a wealthy man, Valentina. Did you think I was kidding."

"How...?" she asked. She knew he was wealthy, but this was still too much, after all, she knew his business inside and out.

"It hit home for me on Christmas day," he said. "Everything you told me was right. I do want to help the town. But I also want time with my wife and son. So I can't do it all myself. And I realized that I know one person who I feel completely at peace handing it off to."

"But, these numbers," she said helplessly, gesturing to the deed.

"I liquidated another project that I didn't feel as strongly about," he said, shrugging.

"The parking lots," she said, horrified, but knowing she had to be right. Radcliffe had bought up several of the structures in the city over the years. "But they were so lucrative, and their value was only going to skyrocket."

"Some things are just more important," he said, shrugging. "I think you're starting to know what I mean."

All at once it hit her that he was talking about Tanner and Zeke.

And then the multiple truths of the situation landed. She didn't work for Radcliffe anymore, she owned the most valuable piece of land in Trinity Falls, and there was no reason at all that she couldn't fall madly in love with Tanner Williams if she wanted to. And if he loved her back, the three of them might just live happily ever after.

Suddenly, she found herself weeping.

"Hey," Radcliffe said, getting up from his chair and coming around the desk to wrap an arm around her shoulders. "Hey, don't cry."

"This is too much," she sobbed.

"No, it's just right," he said gruffly. "The more I thought about this, the more I realize I don't just owe you for the work you've done, I also owe you for the happiness I found with my wife and son."

"That doesn't make any sense," she sniffled. "You already pay me."

"I built an empire, in part because of your ideas and competence," he said. "And if I hadn't known you were holding down the fort here, I couldn't have stepped away long enough to fall in love with Emma. I wouldn't have learned to spend more time with my son."

He meant it, and the realization that there was some truth to what he said touched her heart, which started her crying in earnest all over again.

"M-Mr. Radcliffe," she sobbed.

"Oh, for heaven's sake," he said. "Can't you finally call me Baz now?"

That struck her funny for some reason, and she let out a yelp of laughter even though tears were still sliding down her face.

"Hang on a second," Radcliffe said.

He went to the door and threw it open.

"Tanner Williams," he yelled furiously. "Come in here and get your girl. And Sloane Greenfield, meet me on the stairs, please."

He marched out like he was angry, which only made Valentina laugh harder through her tears. She was pretty sure he just didn't like to see her crying.

A haunted looking Tanner appeared in the doorway a moment later.

"Valentina," he breathed, crouching in front of her chair and gazing at her with real concern, which she figured made sense since she was laughing and crying all at once. "I'm so sorry. I didn't mean to... Are you okay?"

"More than okay," she gasped.

He frowned, but he took her hands in his.

"I know this is a difficult time for you," he said carefully. "And I want to give you all the time in the world to get through it. But remember that rule you had about not dating anyone you work with? Is that the reason...?"

"Yes," she said quickly.

"Yes?" he asked, his eyes flashing to hers.

"Yes, it's the only reason," she said, suddenly feeling shy.

He nodded, his lips pulled up slightly at the corners.

"Valentina, may I take you out for dinner?" he asked, standing and offering her his hand.

"Yes," she said, standing. "But it had better be in that ballroom, because I'm not leaving this wedding."

"I really want to ask you why," Tanner murmured, pulling her close. "But I want to kiss you more."

Her heart fluttered as she went up on her toes and Tanner wrapped his arms around her, brushing her lips gently with his and then kissing her passionately, like he might never stop.

Someone cleared their throat in the doorway, and she pulled back immediately, mortified, but still breathless.

"Ready to sign some papers?" Radcliffe asked.

Sloane Greenfield stood behind him, her eyes sparkling like she wanted to start giggling.

"Very ready," Valentina said.

She could feel Tanner's questioning eyes on her, but she knew she didn't need his approval to sign her name and put an end to the first stage of her career in the most unexpected of ways.

And if everything went like she hoped it would, she would have the rest of their lives to explain it to him.

23

VALENTINA

After an evening of dancing, celebration, and telling a stunned Tanner what had really happened in Baz's makeshift office, Valentina was exhausted and delighted as Tanner walked her to her car.

The stars winked as if they were happy too, and the fresh cold air of the wintry Pennsylvania night felt good on her flushed cheeks. Tanner took her hand in his as they stepped down from the castle porch and into the parking area.

As they walked, it hit Valentina that they were all alone for the first time all night, and she felt shy. She hadn't had a lot of time for dating, or really for anything but working ever since she had taken her job with Baz Radcliffe. She didn't have much experience with dating or kissing, and she knew she didn't really want things getting physical, at least not now. She hoped that was okay with him.

"What's wrong?" Tanner asked, stopping in his tracks.

"Oh, nothing," Valentina said, feeling mortified.

"I know you too well for you to tell me nothing's wrong," he said. "It was a big night, with a lot of changes. Is that it?"

"Kind of," she admitted.

"Sloane said those deeds won't be recorded until she takes them down to the courthouse," he said, squeezing her hand. "We can march right back up there, and you can tell him to keep that land."

"What?" she asked.

"You can go back to the city," he told her. "You can get the kind of job you want, running a business and reporting to a board, or whatever it is you like to do. You don't have to change your whole life just because he's offering. Anyone would be lucky to hire you. And Baz can clean up his own mess here."

"What about us?" she asked softly, feeling stupid the moment the words left her mouth. There was no *us*. They hadn't even been on a single date.

"We'll figure it out," he told her seriously. "I don't want to lose you. But mostly, I don't want you to lose yourself."

Suddenly, tears were sliding down her cheeks again.

"Oh, no," he moaned. "I'm so sorry. What did I say?"

"You always say the right thing, Tanner Williams," she told him, letting go of his hand to wipe the tears from her cheeks. "It never occurred to me to turn him down, because I love it here, and I *do* want to handle the Trinity Falls market project myself."

Tanner smiled at that, his eyes crinkling with warmth.

"But I owe it to my parents to talk to them first," she said, not exactly wanting to give him the details.

He nodded thoughtfully.

"I'll call them tonight," she told him. "Even though it's late."

"Will you tell them about me?" he asked hopefully.

"Yes," she said, smiling up at him. "I'm going to tell them all about you and Zeke."

He wrapped a gentle hand around her still-wet face and stroked the apple of her cheek with his calloused thumb.

"You mean everything to us," he told her. "So we're going to take this slowly."

She nodded, soaking in the heat of his hand and feeling sweet relief. Tanner was really and truly the perfect man.

HALF AN HOUR LATER, she was safely home. She had taken a moment to put on cozy pajamas, and then pulled out her laptop and initiated the video call before she could lose her nerve.

"Valentina?" her mother said sleepily, wiping a hand over her eyes. "Is everything okay?"

"Yes," she replied. "Is Dad there?"

"Where else would he be after ten o'clock at night?" her mother scolded gently. "Hang on. I'll wake him."

"*Vale?*" her father's voice sounding in the background a minute later.

"*She says she's okay,*" her mother whispered back in a

decidedly suspicious way. *"But she's wearing a lot of makeup and her hair is weird."*

"Hang on, honey," her dad called out.

"I was at the wedding, Mom," Valentina reminded her mother. "That's the reason I look like this."

"Okay, baby," her mom said, still sounding worried.

Valentina waited, watching the video feed from her mother's phone screen deliver a topsy turvy montage of blankets and her father's plaid pajamas, a bumpy ride down the staircase, and finally the usual view from the napkin holder her mom used as a phone stand, down in the kitchen.

"Okay, *mi vida*," her dad said. "What's up?"

"My boss is giving me a huge tract of land," she said, cutting right to the chase. "He told me tonight at the wedding. But I can't sell it."

"He's what?" her father asked.

"You can't?" her mom asked at the same time.

"Well, I *could* sell it legally," Valentina said. "But that's not what he wants, and it's not what I want either. This little town..." But it was too hard to explain the place Trinity Falls had won in her heart.

"It's your Manchester," her father finished for her.

"What?" she asked. It was ridiculous to compare the storied Manchester apartment building and its wealthy residents to the down-to-earth people of Trinity Falls.

"I don't mean what it actually is," her father said. "Of course your country village isn't like this building. But you love the people, don't you? They're your community."

"Yes, that's exactly it," she said, still not seeing the connection between the two places, but glad he understood. "If I take this land, I'll basically be a steward for it. I'll earn a living from rents from the organizations that use it, but I won't allow anything to go in that won't benefit the town, so it probably won't be enough to help you. At least not for a while."

"Help us?" her mother asked.

"You both worked so hard all your lives to give Gabriel and Rafe and me a good education," Valentina said softly. "I always hoped one of us could buy you your own condo one day, so Dad wouldn't have to run around fixing people's sinks and changing their lightbulbs forever."

There was absolute silence on the other end of the call, and if she hadn't seen her parents exchanging a look, she might have thought the screen had frozen.

"Oh, honey," her mother said, turning back to her. "I hope that's not why you've been working so hard."

"We could have bought our own place a long time ago, *mi vida*," her father said gently. "After all, we haven't paid rent since before you were born. And we lived as simply as we could."

"Wait... then why are you still there?" Valentina asked in awe.

"I love the Manchester," her father said. "This is our home, our community."

"But they call you twenty-four hours a day," Valentina said, shaking her head. "For things that aren't even emergencies."

"They're our neighbors," her father said sternly, as he had many times over the years, but suddenly she realized he *meant it,* every time. "And most of them are older than we are. They're lonely, and they need our help."

"Besides," her mother said with a smile. "Your father likes to stay busy. Now that you kids are up and running, he gets lonely too."

"Marinela," her father protested.

"Well, it's true, *mi amor,*" she said, leaning over to kiss him on the nose. "We won't leave the Manchester for a long, long time, Vale. And when we do, we've got our own savings. You don't need to worry about Papá and me."

"What's going on?" Rafe asked sleepily from the kitchen doorway.

"Your sister is about to tell us all about her boyfriend," her mother said with a knowing smile.

Valentina's jaw literally dropped.

"Am I wrong?" her mother asked with a smile as her brother made silly cooing noises in the background.

"No," Valentina said with a smile of her own. "I guess not. Although he hasn't taken me out on a single date yet, so I'm not sure how you guessed."

"You missed a Sunday call," her father said wisely. "That's how we knew there was a man."

That actually made a lot of sense.

"I'll keep you posted on him," Valentina promised. "But so far, he's pretty great, and so is his son."

Her brother put on the tea kettle as she began to tell them all about Tanner and Zeke. It was almost as good as being home at the kitchen table herself. And the more they talked and laughed, the more Valentina felt like a huge weight had been lifted from her.

24

VALENTINA

A week later, Valentina rode Emma's horse, Clifford, around the paddock on the Williams Homestead, the wind lifting her hair, and her heart as light as a feather.

When Tanner asked what she wanted to do for their first date, she hadn't been sure. But when he half-jokingly asked if she would like to have a horseback riding lesson on the homestead and then eat dinner with his aunt and uncle and Zeke, she had realized that was *exactly* what she wanted.

And that first lesson went so well that they had been continuing all week after Tanner was finished work each day. She would stop by to sit with Zeke while he did his forty-five minutes of math and Tanner made dinner, and then they would head over to the homestead to ride horses and enjoy each other's company, before the boys dropped her off at the door to her building, then walked across the lawn to theirs.

Baz had brought in another promising young executive from his offices in the city to act as her replacement. And now that she was slowly handing off her work to Darcy, Valentina was a little less busy. Though she was spending an awful lot of time dreaming up ways to use the land that was now at her disposal.

"Go, Valentina, go," Zeke called out to her from where he sat on the fence beside his dad. The radiant smile on his little face filled her heart. "And go, Clifford."

Clifford was Emma's elderly horse from her childhood. He was gentle as could be, but still had just enough gumption to be happy galloping a bit at the end of each lesson. And Valentina spoiled him with a nice brushing and a pocketful of carrots after every cooldown.

What was different about tonight was that they had come here straight after math, without eating. And after they dropped Zeke off at home with his babysitter, Valentina and Tanner were going out for dinner. It would be their first grownups only date.

She would definitely miss her Zeke time tonight. But it was exciting to think about dressing up and going out with her boyfriend.

"What are you smiling about?" Tanner teased as she and Clifford galloped past.

But she only laughed and enjoyed her ride, and the company of her two favorite guys in the world.

AFTER THE LESSON, she went home again, where she showered and put on a pretty dress with some boots that had a sensible heel. It was nice to feel dressed-up without having to put on a suit and pumps.

"Hi," she said to Tanner when she got downstairs.

In spite of all their plans, Zeke was right there by his side, holding a laptop.

"Don't worry," Tanner told her right away. "We're still going to dinner. But we wanted to put the lights on for one last night."

Valentina was surprised that Tanner hadn't taken down all the holiday decorations right after Christmas. She guessed that a lot of people in town didn't get around to that until after New Year's.

But Baz and Emma's New Year's wedding had come and gone, and a week later, he was planning to turn them on again.

"Okay," she said with a smile.

She certainly wasn't going to say no to the beautiful display of lights. And besides, she suspected that maybe the real reason that he hadn't had time to take them down because he was spending all his free time with her.

"Great," he said. "Come on."

He took her hand and Zeke hopped along beside them, so she wrapped her free arm around his shoulders.

"You sit here, Valentina," Zeke said, pointing to one of the two stone benches in the center of the display.

She did as she was told, wondering what was going on when Tanner moved to take the laptop and set it on the opposite bench, opening it up and tapping a few keys. The familiar sound of a video call ringing followed, and then the distinct sound of her father's voice.

"Tanner, is that you?" he asked.

"Where's Zeke?" her mother's voice followed.

"Here I am," Zeke squealed, capering over to wave at the screen.

Of course Valentina had included Tanner and Zeke in her most recent family call, which went on long enough that Valentina had ducked out to start dinner. But she didn't expect Tanner to be calling her parents himself. She certainly hadn't shared their number.

He stepped aside, allowing her to see that it wasn't just her parents. Rafe and Gabriel were there too in their own rectangles, all of them observing her with knowing smiles.

Zeke sat beside her, his little hand wrapping around hers.

"Valentina," Tanner said, drawing her attention up to him. "I know I said that I would take things slowly because you're so important to Zeke and to me."

Something began to occur to her, and she glanced at the computer screen, but her whole family was watching Tanner.

"But I just can't wait any longer," Tanner went on. "I've spoken with your father, and if you say yes, we have his blessing."

"Dad," she murmured, her eyes back on the screen.

Her father winked at her, but even through the video feed, she could see that his eyes were glistening.

"From the day I met you, I knew you were special," Tanner said. "You listen to me, and you care so much about everyone and everything you touch. And the way you love my son takes my breath away."

"Valentina," Zeke said, suddenly hopping up from the

bench. "I want you to be my mama. I want to teach you how to go on hikes and ride horses, and you'll teach me how to help people. I... I want you to be in my family, *please*."

The first part had obviously been something he'd thought about ahead of time. But when he asked her to be in his family, she could hear the real note of pleading in his voice and she wrapped her arms around him, holding him close, unable to speak for fear she would start crying.

"Valentina Jimenez," Tanner said, kneeling and holding up a little wooden box with a shimmering ring nestled inside. "We promise to love you forever. Will you be my wife, and join our family?"

"Yes," she said quickly.

"*Yes,*" Zeke cheered, letting go of her and jumping up and down.

Her family cheered right along with him, and her tears finally broke, sliding down her cheeks as joy filled her heart.

Tanner was smiling at her with tears in his own eyes as he slid the delicate band around her finger.

He lifted his eyebrows as if to ask her permission before leaning in to kiss her, in full view of the laptop. It was a chaste kiss that still sent a shiver down her spine.

Then her brother made kissy noises that made Zeke laugh so hard he started hiccupping.

But Valentina didn't have a care in the world. She might not have gotten her parents a house, but she had brought them a son-in-law and a grandson.

She had spent a lifetime chasing worldly success. But

the most important thing that could ever happen to her had been given to her freely. She would never take that for granted.

"A penny for your thoughts," Tanner said softly, as Zeke talked a mile a minute to her parents.

"I was just thinking how happy I am," she told him.

"Thank you," he told her, his deep voice breaking with emotion. "Thank you for agreeing to marry me. I'll spend the rest of my life trying to make you glad you did."

"So, when's the wedding?" Valentina's dad boomed from the laptop.

Tanner's eyes crinkled with mirth and Valentina smiled too.

"As soon as she'll have me, sir," Tanner said. "And as soon as all of you can be here."

Everyone started talking about flights and schedules and best times for weddings, but Valentina just took it all in. She knew the details didn't matter. Everything that mattered to her was right in front of her, on either side of that little screen.

25

VALENTINA

V alentina took one last look around her old office at Radcliffe's farmhouse.

It looked so different without the framed family photo from her fifteenth birthday, her grandfather's horse statue, and her other little memories and decorations. But the space would serve Darcy well, and she would surely have her own personal items to brighten up the space.

Darcy was bright and cheerful, and she seemed to have great instincts and a killer work ethic. Although her outgoing energy contrasted with Valentina's more reserved personality, Valentina liked her very much. Darcy would take good care of the ongoing tasks for the land project now that Valentina was moving on. And since she wasn't moving far, Valentina knew she could always lend an ear or a hand if Darcy needed it.

Today, Darcy was on site for a roof project. It was sad not to have a proper hand off on Valentina's last official day, but she was glad that her replacement had already rolled up her sleeves and gotten to work.

Grabbing the container she had brought in this morning, and her empty coffee cup, Valentina headed down to the old barn for the last time.

The wood that had been laid over the muddy ground was gone for some reason. But it didn't really matter, since she wore boots every day now, and the pretty lavender coverall from Tanner too, if she was on a particularly messy site.

The container she held was still warm. She had put oatmeal raisin cookies in the oven this morning. They were a big favorite with the guys, and she was hoping to leave on a high note. Though honestly, the workers might not even remember she was going, or that today was her last day. They all had their own crews and friends. There was no way for them to know that for most of the first year she'd spent in Trinity Falls, going to the barn in the mornings wasn't just a way to do her job better, it was her main social activity.

Now she had more social activities than she knew what to do with. To her immense relief, Emma and her friends thought it was hysterical that she had pretended she already knew how to ride a horse. Maybe because Valentina was capable at other things, it humanized her for them to know she most definitely wasn't capable at everything—even something all of them had known how to do since childhood.

They had taken to inviting her out for girls' nights, and she had mustered the courage to accept. She was starting to really feel like she was a part of their crew.

But of course her favorite days were the ones she spent with Tanner and Zeke. They hadn't nailed down a wedding date yet, but her parents had a few options for travel dates in the spring, when her mother could take vacation time, and Valentina hoped that by Easter, she would be an official part of the Williams family at last.

She looked around at the sepia-toned Pennsylvania ridge opposite the farm. This place had a haunting beauty she would definitely miss. But there were so many wonderful things waiting for her on the beautiful tract of land that she hoped to turn into something magical for the town.

And there was something wonderful about having a project that would *really* be all her own.

Tanner's cousin Brad was moving home for good. He was an important architect in the city, but he had agreed that the Trinity Falls open air market would be his first project back home. Hiring Brad had already moved up the timeframe on the project exponentially. Valentina couldn't wait to see all her ideas become a reality for the town she loved so much.

As she got closer to the barn, she saw that it was dark inside. Which was odd, since the big doors were generally open in the mornings.

She stepped inside, and suddenly the whole barn was illuminated.

"*Surprise,*" a chorus of voices cried.

"Oh," Valentina gasped. "Oh, wow."

All the crews were there, not just the morning regulars she saw every day. Everyone had plastic cups of what looked like apple cider. And there were picnic tables set up in the barn.

Daniel Sullivan came over and shook her hand.

"We're going to miss you," he told her.

"And not just the treats," Kevin Anderson said over his shoulder.

"Guys," she said, feeling tears prickle her eyes. "I can't believe you would do this for me."

"You listen to us every morning," Leroy Gregory said gruffly, running a paint-stained hand through his shock of white hair. "And you try to help solve our problems. That means a lot, young lady."

When he offered her his hand, she found herself pulling him in for a hug, which made him chuckle.

"So, you knew why I was really coming down here?" she asked the men who had gathered around her.

"It wasn't just to pawn off your cookies," Luke Anderson said. "Though my brother here would have been just fine with that."

Kevin elbowed Luke and the two of them laughed.

"Of course we knew," Daniel said gently. "And we appreciated it. Why do you think we put that wood down?"

It hit her suddenly that the wood hadn't just appeared mysteriously. They put it down for her, because the crews wanted her here, listening and advocating for them. And they hadn't wanted her to break her ankle in her high heels while she was doing it.

"I was so lucky to work here with you," she said, shaking her head and blinking back tears.

Someone handed her a cup of cider, and the guys all

came up, patting her on the back and shaking her hand, congratulating her on her upcoming project and on her engagement to Tanner.

The phrases *great guy* and *lucky guy* got tossed around so many times that she lost count.

Valentina hadn't realized how much she worried that deep down, they were only being polite, and that no one really wanted a city girl running things. But now she knew for sure that they didn't think that way at all. The men she had come to respect and admire seemed to feel just the same way about her.

"Hope you all don't mind that I'm going to say a few words while Mrs. Luckett and her crew bring in the refreshments," a deep, familiar voice said.

Everyone quieted and turned as Baz Radcliffe came forward to speak.

When he stepped into view, Valentina suddenly realized that Tanner and Zeke had been standing in the corner with Emma, watching proudly as she had her big moment. That knowledge made an already sweet experience all the more memorable.

"I'm glad everyone could be here," he said with a big smile. "I feel for anyone in Trinity Falls who needs work done on their property today."

The sound of chuckles and laughter filled the space.

"I'd like to take a moment to formally welcome you to the Farewell and Happy Engagement Party for Valentina Jimenez," he went on. "I've spent a long time in business, and I've worked with some of the smartest people in the world, and some of the luckiest. But no matter how successful, I've never met anyone like our Valentina."

She felt her cheeks warm, but she managed to keep her eyes on her boss and mentor.

"Because Valentina isn't just smart," he went on. "And she hasn't just made a few lucky calls. She's loyal to a fault, and she truly cares about doing the right thing. This is a woman who makes deals by listening, and who knows how to create a win-win out of any negotiation— because if you sit down with her, she's not going to get up until she understands you."

"Hear, hear," one of the men hollered. Others chuckled and made sounds of agreement.

"This is a bittersweet day for me," he went on. "Bitter not because I'm losing her work ethic and her smarts, but because I know Valentina as a person, as a friend, and I'll miss seeing her every day."

She swallowed over the lump in her throat, knowing she would miss seeing Baz, Wes, and Emma too.

"And sweet because nothing is sweeter than being inspired by a young person and seeing them exceed your wildest dreams of what they can become," he said, nodding to her. "Congratulations, Valentina. We can't wait to see what you make of the Valentine Corporation's land tract, and we're thrilled to see you find happiness with one of our own, Tanner Williams, and his son, Zeke. To your future!"

"To your future," the others called out, raising their plastic cups of apple cider to her.

She lifted her own cup and drank deep.

Then everyone was looking at her, as if she was supposed to make her own speech.

"I don't know how to follow that," she said honestly.

That won her an unexpected laugh.

"But I'll try," she said gamely, facing Radcliffe. "Anything I do with my future career, any success I find, it will be because you took an interest in me, and because you had the patience to answer every question I had, for *years.*"

He smiled at that.

"And if I ever fall down," she went on. "It will be because I didn't listen to your voice in my head, reminding me of what's important. Thank you to every single person in this room for helping me learn the right way to run a farm and a business here in Trinity Falls."

The guys clapped and Emma winked at her from beside Baz.

"I owe my happiness to you and Emma for putting me in Tanner's path and him in mine," she went on, facing her boss and his new wife again. "He and Zeke have taught me how to let my hair down a little, and how to enjoy life, and how to love without asking for anything in return…"

She broke down a little, tears trying to escape her eyes. After a few deep breaths, she pulled herself back together.

"Well," Valentina went on, laughing at herself a little. "You all know me. You know how much these two have changed pretty much everything for me."

Murmurs of understanding and appreciation went through the gathering. Tanner's eyes met hers and she felt like she was being warmed from the inside out under his gaze.

"I'm going to miss every one of you here at the farm,"

she said, wrapping up. "But don't worry, I'm sure I'll be back to say hello to all of you and to visit the best boss a person could have. You can't get rid of me that easily, not even by firing me, Baz."

She winked at him, wondering if he noticed that she had finally used his first name. When he strode up and wrapped her in a big hug, she knew he had.

"*Valentina, Valentina,*" Zeke cried, running up to her. "I have a surprise for you."

"Hey, *mi vida,*" she said, crouching down to meet him. "What is it?"

"Look," he said reverently, handing her a little remote control. "Push the button."

She glanced up and saw that Tanner was there with him, gazing down at her with that look that told her she was longed for, adored, and treasured.

"Okay," she said. "Here we go. Three, two..."

"*One,*" Zeke yelled along with her.

She pressed the button and suddenly the whole ceiling of the barn was filled with soft light. She looked up to see that Tanner had strung fairy lights from every beam and rafter of the massive structure, making it feel like they were under a sky of shimmering stars.

Someone started strumming the chords of an old classic rock tune on the acoustic guitar, and she was stunned to see it was Bud, the head of the paint crew. Daniel Sullivan joined in, playing the melody on a fiddle and she looked to Tanner, amazed.

"May I have this dance?" he asked.

She looked down to Zeke, not wanting to leave him out. But he was already running off with Baz's son, Wes.

"Yes," she said, smiling.

He took her in his arms, and she had never felt such happiness. All around them, their friends were chatting. Now that she had the time to look around a little, she could see that Holly Fields from the café was here too, and Caroline and Logan, and so many others—people who clearly already saw her as a part of their community.

Mrs. Luckett and a few of her contemporaries were carrying out so much food. And Annabelle Williams set a beautiful cake down on one of the tables.

"It's so beautiful," Valentina breathed, "seeing everyone here together."

"Alone we can do so little, together we can do so much," he said. "A wise man once told me that."

"Was that wise man my father?" she asked him, smiling at the familiar, yet beloved words.

"Yes," Tanner said.

"And I think he was quoting Helen Keller," she added. "But it's true in this situation."

"Your dad has collected some really good words of wisdom," he said, nodding.

"He's been around longer than we have," she pointed out. "We've got plenty more time to gather wisdom, and plenty of friends to gather it with—more than I ever realized."

"I know I've got everything I could ever need right here," Tanner said, his voice rough with emotion.

When he bent to kiss her, she could see their whole world unfolding in her mind—suppers with Zeke, adventures in the winter snow and the summer sun, evenings on the porch sitting in rocking chairs, watching the fireflies flicker just like the twinkling ceiling of the barn tonight, lighting up her heart, the way her love for her husband and son and their beautiful community always would.

***

Thanks for reading **Cowboy's Christmas Bridesmaid!**

Want to read Tanner and Valentina's **SPECIAL BONUS EPILOGUE**? Sign up for my newsletter here (or just enter your email if you're already signed up!):
https://www.clarapines.com/christmasbrides
maidbonus.html

About the next book:

Do you remember little Josie, who helped her uncle Logan find love with Caroline in *Cowboy's Christmas Librarian*? Well, her dad, Brad Williams, is finally coming home to settle down in Trinity Falls with Josie for good. Do you want to find out what happens when he suddenly realizes that the woman he brings with him has become so much more than just his daughter's nanny?

Then be sure to grab **Architect's Christmas Nanny!**

www.clarapines.com/architectsnanny

ABOUT THE AUTHOR

Clara Pines is a writer from Pennsylvania. She loves writing sweet romance, sipping peppermint tea with her handsome husband, and baking endless gingerbread cookies with her little helpers. A holiday lover through and through, Clara wishes it could be Christmas every day. You can almost always figure out where she has curled up to write by following the sound of the holiday music on her laptop!

Get all the latest info, and join Clara's mailing list at:

www.clarapines.com

Plus, you'll get the chance for sneak peeks of upcoming titles and other cool stuff!

Keep in touch...
www.clarapines.com
authorclarapines@gmail.com
Tiktok.com/authorclarapines

facebook.com/ClaraPinesAuthor

x.com/clarapines

instagram.com/authorclarapines

Made in the USA
Las Vegas, NV
13 December 2024